Cady

Also by Lillian Eige

The Kidnapping of Mister Huey

Cady

Lillian Eige

illustrations by Janet Wentworth

For Meaghan
Happy reading!
Lillian Eige
December 1, 1992

1 8 🔥 1 7

HARPER & ROW, PUBLISHERS

Cambridge, Philadelphia, San Francisco, Washington, London, Mexico City, São Paolo, Singapore, Sydney

NEW YORK

Cady

Copyright © 1987 by Lillian Eige

Designed by Joyce Hopkins

1 2 3 4 5 6 7 8 9 10

First Edition

Library of Congress Cataloging-in-Publication Data
Eige, Lillian.
  Cady.

  Summary: Having been shuffled from one relative to
another all his life, twelve-year-old Cady eventually
finds acceptance and love in a foster home and an
understanding of the father he has never known.
  [1. Foster home care—Fiction.   2. Fathers and sons—
Fiction]   I. Wentworth, Janet, ill.   II. Title.
PZ7.E3437Cad 1987   [Fic]   85-45818
ISBN 0-06-021792-8
ISBN 0-06-021793-6 (lib. bdg.)

For my family,
Gay, and Jon and Julie

Cady

1

Shortly before midnight, in the middle of a pouring rain, old Gran died. Cady was standing in the doorway of the kitchen watching when the doctor came. He saw the doctor shake his head. It was springtime, not a time for dying, Cady thought. He stared out the window into the blackness. The rain kept falling and the house was cold. There was no one to talk to. The Hawk had started screaming and crying, and she wouldn't stop.

Cady went to his room and stuffed a rug under the door to shut out the sound. He crawled into bed with all of his clothes on, and pulled the covers over his head. He still shivered. He couldn't stay on here now that old Gran was dead. He had come two years ago when he was nine. Until then he had been passed from one relative to another, handed around like a hot piece of stolen goods, a game of hide-and-seek. He had made that observation by the time he was nine. Then, without warning, he had been packed up and delivered to old Gran to help care for her.

Gran was a tiny thing, sharp tongued and shrill, her memory failing then. She had the musty smell of age, and her eyes watered. "That him?" she asked, seeing Cady for the first time. She peered at him out of pale eyes. She rarely talked to him after that.

Old Gran lived with her cat, Libby, in a dingy old house. She kept the curtains pulled day and night, and she slept on a cot in the kitchen beside the stove. Cady slept in a faraway corner at the top of the house. They ate mostly toast and poached eggs, and liver shared with the cat. Sometimes when he was lonely, Cady sneaked old Libby up to his room. He let the cat lie on the bed with him and crawl up on his chest, making a waterfall of fur whenever she moved.

When old Gran screamed in the night, when she was having a raving fit, Cady wrapped his arms around her, laying his cheek gently against Gran's. She didn't know who Cady was most of the time, and she spit at him like a startled animal.

His aunt Josephine came to live with old Gran the next year when Cady was eleven. She seemed almost as old as Gran, but she was tall, heavy and domineering. She had a pinched mouth and a crooked nose that buckled in the middle. She told him she was his mother's older sister, and to call her Aunty. He never did. Because of the way she acted and looked, he called her the Hawk. Cady imagined the Hawk raising up on huge wings, her long ungainly legs hanging limp.

Her husband had disappeared into thin air, she declared. "Hateful man," she called him. It became a secret pleasure for Cady to visualize a whole man vanishing into the air, and the shock of it to the Hawk. She also called Cady's father the most despicable man on earth to run off the way he did. "But you don't need to worry about him," she said. "He's probably dead. Nobody ever heard from him again." Cady knew that it pleased her to say that. She rolled it around on her tongue like a bite of chocolate.

It was the Hawk who explained all about the birds and the bees to Cady. One night, she spoke of his birth. "You were the death of your mother," she said. "My poor baby sister." It was hard for Cady to think in terms of death about his mother. He had seen pictures of her. She was pretty and gentle looking, a young girl. He had not known that she died giving birth to him.

That night Cady went out behind the house and cried himself sick, vomiting until he couldn't hold up his head. It was then Cady began to notice how different old Gran and the Hawk were from him. It was their dark skin, and hair. He was conscious of his own reddish hair and light skin. Whenever he heard the screaming between old Gran and the Hawk, he tried not to listen. The Hawk complained that he was lazy, that Cady didn't help her. She compared him to his father.

Cady didn't believe the lies the Hawk told about his father, but for as long as he could remember, wherever he had lived, no one would answer his questions or speak of him. They pretended not to know. So he quit asking, and he made up stories to suit himself: His father was a hero in the Secret Service, or a spy traveling all over the world for his country.

That would explain his being away from Cady. Sometimes he had dreams about his father, and they were together. He had expected to grow up like him until the Hawk tried to ruin it for Cady. By the time he was twelve, a running battle continued between Cady and the Hawk, mainly because he screamed "Hawk" at her now whenever she mentioned his dad.

Old Gran and Libby slept out their days on the cot in the kitchen. It got so that Cady had to tell old Gran who he was every day, and then she paid no attention to him. Sometimes it was hard for Cady to know if Gran and the cat were dead or alive in the morning light. And now old Gran was dead.

Cady slept little during the night. Early in the morning he started a fire in the stove. It was only Libby alone on the cot now. She hadn't even moved. The cat didn't care about old Gran dying. Cady made coffee, and pushed the cat down in front of a dish of milk.

"You taking over now?" He turned around. His aunt Josephine teetered into the room. Her face was puffed from crying, but she actually smiled at Cady. "There will be people here today," she said. She had on a purple dress and long stockings, instead of the anklets she usually wore. Her hair was brushed back behind her ears into a knot. She started setting the table. "I'm going to let you stay, if you behave." Cady saw that she was smirking. "It's my house now. You want to stay—don't you?" She checked Cady's fire in the stove. "Did you make your bed?"

Cady shook his head and flung his hair from his

face. For a second his half-closed eyes caught his aunt's. He didn't speak.

"Don't you look at me that way."

"What way?" Cady began to laugh.

His aunt charged at him like a madwoman. "Don't you laugh at me! And don't get the idea you're going anywhere. You're not running away from me!" She slapped him hard enough to make his lip bleed. "You act just like him sometimes. Don't try running off like he did. My poor sister." She turned and cried bitterly.

"Why do you want me here, then?" The hate inside Cady was like a hard knot under his breastbone.

"Get the kitchen mess cleaned up, and the cat out of here before the minister comes." She blew her nose hard, and wiping her eyes, she said, "You can do that much."

It rained all that day, streaming against the school windows. He had run off to school that morning just to get away from the house. Maybe it wasn't expected, with a death in the family, but Cady didn't care.

It was still pouring when Cady came out of school. He was surprised at the flooding. When he found the footbridge across from the school grounds washed out, he tried to leap over the creek. He slipped and fell into the water. At first he was completely submerged. He fought to get his head up. He heard someone yelling at him, but he was carried rapidly away downstream. He struggled, several times going under, then he began to tread water and it became easier to stay afloat. He was swept into a toppled tree at the point where the creek emptied into the Missouri River. Cady crept deep into the branches that were

7

out of the water, and slept there that night.

The next morning he hiked over to Highway 71 and held out his thumb. The first to stop was an old man in a camper. "Where you going, boy?"

"I'd like to get to Springfield." It was the only place that Cady knew to go—where his cousin Marrietta lived.

"You're in luck. I'm pointed in that direction. Jump in."

The old man was unshaven, and he wore a cowboy hat with a three-inch brim. He talked constantly while Cady nodded half asleep in the warm cab. He said it was lonesome traveling alone. His wife was dead and he didn't want to ever go home again. His kids didn't care all that much about what he did. So far he had been in forty states. He'd make 'em all before he was done. The old man cleared his throat and spat out the window. Cady ate the man's cookies and bananas and listened.

He spent two chilly nights with the old man, wrapped in a filthy blanket the man tossed to him. Sometimes when Cady couldn't get to sleep, he watched the old man. His mouth dropped open, and his eyes protruded like two marbles under his thin lids. He looked quite dead when he slept. Cady wondered about Gran—if they had put her in a casket and buried her by this time. He was sorry he'd missed the funeral.

He left the old man in Springfield, in spite of his asking Cady to come along to Texas with him. He did take a sack of bananas the old man offered him.

The address of his cousin Marrietta was firmly in his mind. But as it turned out, the address from her Christmas card wasn't right. "She's moved." A little girl was sitting on the steps of the house eating an apple. "Where?" Cady felt as though the wind had been knocked out of him. A shrill voice came through the door. "I just sent a letter on a couple of days ago, 210 Fleet Street. It's a long way from here." After getting the directions, he walked more than ten miles to find her—it took him half a day. He stopped twice in parks for a drink of water and to eat a banana. It was nighttime and the street lights were coming on before he reached her.

Marrietta lived on the second floor of a rambling old rooming house. It was set right on the street, and it was so noisy from the cars going by, Cady had a hard time getting the woman on the porch to understand him. "I'm looking for Marrietta Brogan," he said. He kept his fingers crossed behind his back.

"Straight up the stairs and to your left." The woman was cross-eyed, and he couldn't tell if she was looking at him.

Before he knocked, he wiped his face with his sleeve and brushed his hair with his hand. He hadn't bathed in three days. Marrietta opened the door only a crack, and peeked around the corner at him. Cady knew her in an instant. She was thin and quick as a wren, and her wispy blond hair lay in bangs across her frightened eyes. She still had an uncared-for look.

As Cady looked at her he remembered what a good friend she had been when he had stayed with her family. The winter he was six they had shared a bed, sleeping spoon fashion, her knees up against his bottom, keeping him warm. And when he had one of his bad dreams, she hugged him tight enough to choke him until his shaking stopped. Later, when he had moved to old Gran's and Marrietta left home, she sent him Christmas cards, signed, "All my love, X X X X, Marrietta." She had also sent him birthday gifts the last two years, both times jigsaw puzzles. And after each birthday he had written her a long letter, thanking her and pouring out every crazy thing that had happened to him the whole year. He signed it, "Love," but he left off the Xs after the second letter. Marrietta was only six years older than he was. "And already saddled with her backward child and no husband. It's a scandal and a disgrace!" The Hawk had carried on every time one of Marrietta's letters came.

Marrietta didn't recognize Cady at first. When she did, she backed away from him. Her eyes brimmed over with tears, and she put her hands over her mouth. "You're not Cady. You can't possibly be Cady. You're dead—you're drowned!"

He stepped in quickly. "I'm Cady. Look at me. You'd better believe it. And I'm not drowned. It's a mistake."

She was quick to explain she had read the news on the back sheet of the *Springfield Tribune*, one small paragraph. "They said you were missing, they thought you drowned. Someone saw you go under, and they didn't see you again. They looked and looked for you." She grabbed him around the neck, and her tears flowed down his shirt front. She told him he was one of the few people she considered a real true friend, and she had been all broken up ever since she read it.

Cady was extremely pleased at finding himself drowned, and Marrietta sobbing her heart out over

10

him. "I'm not drowned," Cady said again, "but I hope they keep looking." He shut the door behind him.

Marrietta scooped up Jenny and held her toward Cady. The child's face was slightly lopsided, and her eyes heavy lidded, slanting almost shut.

"Hello, Jenny," Cady said. It didn't bother him about the little girl's looks. He took her hand.

"She doesn't talk." In a little flurry Marrietta hugged Jenny and kissed the top of her head. She suddenly looked up to see how Cady was taking it. "She's my funny bunny. She's not like any other kid on earth." There was a look of awful pain on Marrietta's face. It struck Cady it might be sympathy for him, too. He felt as if his spine had suddenly melted. He was terribly tired and frightened.

So Cady stayed on. Marrietta let him have Jenny's daybed and she took Jenny in to sleep with her. They went to a church rummage sale the next day and bought Cady two pairs of jeans and two shirts and a sweater. They lived mostly on welfare and food stamps. Cady started working at odd jobs, mowing lawns and weeding. He turned all his money over to Marrietta. When she worked extra waiting on tables in the Busy Bee, he took care of Jenny and did the cooking. Jenny, three years old, couldn't speak a word or walk by herself, but Cady could make her laugh—small explosions that came bursting to the surface like the fizz from soda pop. He carried her from place to place so she could be near him. When Marrietta worked late, he rocked Jenny. In the darkest part of the night he talked to her about being alone, and belonging nowhere. Jenny slept on peacefully, her mouth puckered in a smile.

In the summer they went to the park on Sundays and let Jenny sit in the sun. When they had money enough on hot days, they swam in the public pool. No one bothered them or gave them an extra glance. If they had asked questions, Marrietta would have said, "My brother."

By fall Cady's grass-mowing jobs were over and Marrietta had no work at the Busy Bee. Once in a while she got a baby-sitting job. When winter came and they were closed in, she taught him to dance. "I love to dance," she said. "It lifts me." She looked slightly wild to Cady as she twirled about the room to the radio, showing him how. So on winter nights, holding Jenny between them to keep warm, the three children swayed to the music, their shadows like dancing dolls on the walls.

One night at the beginning of summer it suddenly ended. Marrietta, mysterious and frightened, told him he had to leave. When he asked why, it was the same old story—she became upset and shook her head. "I can't tell you any more—please don't ask me."

"But I'm not going back to the Hawk's?"

"No—no. You're going to Thea's. She lives in Minnesota. Don't ask me."

Cady was deeply hurt. His pride wouldn't allow him to ask her again. He went in the middle of the night. Marrietta helped him pack her old suitcase. She insisted on walking to the bus with him. He carried Jenny in his arms, not wanting to let go of her. At the station Marrietta bought his ticket. Cady wondered where the money came from. When the bus was ready to leave, Marrietta kissed him and hung on to him like a little kid. She was trembling. "Don't you be getting mad, or feeling sad and think I don't like you, 'cause I do, more than anybody in the whole world." Her voice was ragged. "We're just poor lost children." She tried to laugh.

She took Jenny out of his arms. "Just remember the name, Thea McVey. You get off the bus a mile past Moravia, Minnesota, at the crossroads. It's going to be a long trip." She patted the sack she had given him. "Some food for you." Marrietta was crying now. "Jenny's going to miss you." She leaned through the door still talking to him. "It's all right for you to go, or else I wouldn't let you." She lowered her voice to a whisper. "If they ask you, say you're fifteen, at least. Don't tell anybody nothing about where you're from."

Cady sat and waved to her through the window. When she was out of sight he leaned back in the seat. He had a sick feeling. He felt the brush of tears across his eyes, but by blinking fast he made them disappear. He doubled up his fist and hit at the seat until his hand ached.

He finally slept toward morning. He was awakened when the bus pulled into the station at Des Moines, Iowa. Hungry, he opened the brown bag and took out a sandwich. When they drove on, Cady looked out the window without seeing the countryside. Instead he saw the faces of Marrietta and Jenny, and he tried not to think about another strange place. He changed buses at Minneapolis, and he had to wait for an hour for another bus to Moravia.

The driver sighed when Cady told him that he wanted to get off a mile past Moravia at the crossroads. The bus was empty except for a woman and a child, and one old man. Cady opened the brown sack and took out his last peanut butter sandwich. He had one apple and a banana left. Wrapped with his sandwich he found a small sealed envelope and a ten-dollar bill. The envelope was addressed to Thea McVey.

He held the ten-dollar bill close to his face, looking at it for a long time. It smelled like the Cashmere Bouquet soap that Marrietta kept in her drawer to perfume her underwear. He folded it and put it in his wallet. Ten dollars from Marrietta, who couldn't pay her rent sometimes.

They passed through Moravia so fast that Cady hardly had a glimpse of the town. And just as suddenly the bus stopped, throwing him against the seat in front of him. The driver was nodding at him. "You the kid that wanted out at the crossroads? This must be the place. Get your shirt on—we're moving out."

Cady jumped out the door with his suitcase. He walked across the road to the mailbox. "Thea McVey," he read out loud. He saw the only path back through a field. It was grassy and fairly wide, a wall of wheat on either side. Cady picked up his suitcase and started running down the path. It led toward a clump of pines that rose up from the wheat like one giant weed, attaching itself to the sky.

2

After a few moments he slowed to a walk. Once he turned around to go back. He put his suitcase down and sat on it. Cady wondered why he had come, blindly following Marrietta's instructions. But if he couldn't trust Marrietta, there would be no one he could trust. He thought of leaving his suitcase here in case he wanted to get away in a hurry. But if someone stole it he would have no clothes. When he started again he remembered the Hawk, and that made it easier to keep going.

At the end of the lane he saw the old house. L shaped, it sprawled half hidden among the trees, as if it had grown there like a mushroom. On the wide front porch a swing moved back and forth in the wind, as if pushed by an unseen hand. A jumble of columbine, spiderwort and ferns grew around the foundation. The carelessness of a wild grapevine draped around the door, and growing into a nearby tree, eased some of Cady's fear. He noticed, too, the violets growing on either side of the path to the house, and the moss-covered bricks. Cady ducked when a robin swooped out of a nest over the door. The whole place had a rakish feel to it that made Cady more comfortable.

There was no sign of anyone about, but Cady had the uneasy feeling of being watched. Then he noticed the small round window in the door, and the face behind it. He heard someone tugging on the other side. A voice said, "Push, the door's stuck. I don't use it much."

The door suddenly gave. A tall woman was waiting. Her eyes looked startled at first but then became calmer as she and Cady stared at each other for what seemed like a full minute. He took a deep breath. "I'm Cady. I was supposed to come here." He handed her the note addressed to Thea McVey.

After reading it, she folded it carefully. "I've been expecting you." Her eyes didn't move from his. They were searching and prodding now, as if she were trying to examine his thoughts. She did not smile, nor was she unfriendly, but Cady saw the strain in her face. "I'm Thea," she said. Her voice was deep, and she wore jeans and a sloppy sweatshirt.

Without another word she picked up his bag and led him back through the house. There were yellow walls, and bare floors almost golden from polishing, covered with bright-colored rugs. Cady saw none of the darkness of old Gran's house. More of the fear that had traveled with him relaxed. In the kitchen was a large round table and a wood-burning range. The room seemed bursting with cupboards. There were no curtains, and the late-afternoon sun came through the layers of pine trees close to the house, painting the room in ripples of light. Cady thought it was like looking into the depths of a pool. It was quiet and peaceful. She asked him if he would like to wash, pointing to the sink and a towel.

When he had finished she told him to sit down. The table was set for two. She filled a bowl with thick beef stew and noodles, and passed him bread still warm. Cady was surprised at how hungry he was. He tried to eat without making noise. He glanced at her from time to time. He sensed the woman's control, her tenseness. Her hair was long and thick, and hung over her shoulders. He heard sparrows chirping outside the window, but the quietness of the woman filled the room and somehow cut out sound. He could feel her watching him.

After all his stew was eaten he put his hands in his lap. At first his eyes traveled around the room, quick as a hummingbird's hovering. But he grew braver, turning his head slightly to meet her eyes. He waited. Her eyes had a burning in them that was hard to read. Her face was bony, with high cheekbones and a strong jaw.

"Well!" she said finally. She leaned forward, resting both elbows on the edge of the table. "I'm sorry that I wasn't there at the road to meet you. I intended to be, but the bus was early." Then she plunged into what seemed the middle of things to Cady. "It's too bad you went to Marrietta's—and then had to leave."

"I had no place else to go." Cady thought of Marrietta—of her tears when he left, of her actions no more sure than Jenny's or his. They had been three children. "Anyway she let me stay," Cady said.

"I wish you had come here. If I had known earlier . . . " She pressed her hair back from her temples. Her hair was red and dark, making her face appear pale.

"Nobody told me where I should go. And I didn't need them to tell me." Cady shook his head emphatically.

"Maybe you didn't." Cady thought she was ready to smile, but she didn't.

"And besides, Marrietta wanted me. She didn't mind at all. She asked me to stay." Cady had almost forgotten that Marrietta had also asked him to leave.

As if she had picked his thoughts out of the air, Thea said, "She couldn't help it. It was something about the welfare department. They were asking questions about you, why you were living there, and who you were. I asked her not to tell them anything." Thea poured him a cup of tea and put a plate of cookies in front of him. "Have you been going to school?"

"Not when I lived with Marrietta."

"But you were in school before that?"

"Yes."

"Did you make good grades?" Thea smiled.

"I tried." Cady's face flushed. He didn't like her questioning him.

"I'll help you with your schoolwork." She hesitated. "If you want me to."

Cady thought about it. "Maybe," he said.

"You're thin. You're not very big for twelve. Did Marrietta have enough to feed you?" Her voice softened. "Little Jenny . . . how is she? Is she well taken care of?"

"Jenny had good care, and we had enough to eat.

19

Marrietta and I worked when we could. I mowed lawns and shoveled snow, and she worked at the Busy Bee. I'm just naturally thin, ma'am."

"Yes, Marrietta would take good care of Jenny." She studied him for a moment. "Call me Thea, please." She started to stack the dishes. Reaching for his bowl, she said, "Cady, what last name do you go by?"

Cady was surprised she asked. "My own. You must know what my name is, Cady Nicholson." He was angry. She seemed to know all about him, so why did she ask?

"They call you that in school?"

"Yes."

"So you took your grandmother's name?"

"I guess so."

"That's too bad. That's not your name." She spoke quietly.

"It's the one I've had all my life."

"Your name is Cady Myerling. It's a good name. If you are going to stay here, you use that name." She sat again, opposite him. She clasped her hands tightly together, and the bones showed through white.

Cady took a deep breath. The unfamiliar name, Myerling, seemed to echo from the walls. He wanted to put his hands over his ears so he wouldn't hear her say it again. What right did she have to change his name? And where did she get it? If she was waiting for him to ask, she needn't hold her breath. He held his face as still as possible to hide his feelings.

It was a cool day, but there were beads of sweat on Thea's upper lip. Her hair fell limp against her cheek. "Do you wonder who I am?"

Cady met her eyes. "Yes, I wonder how come you

know Marrietta, and Jenny—and about me."

"I am a friend of your family." She paused, thinking. "With a special interest in you. We'll leave it at that," she said flatly. She sat quietly, her eyes moving across the room, through the walls, maybe back to Missouri, Cady thought. At least for a few minutes she wasn't in the room. Finally, she said, "I have been here for a long time—anyway it seems long. This was my grandfather's farm. I inherited it. It's a good place to live, for what I do. I used to teach, but now I write. I'll probably stay here."

"When I was with Marrietta—that was the longest time I stayed with anyone except old Gran," Cady volunteered. "She's dead."

"Yes, I know." Thea's voice sharpened. "And then you disappeared, too, thought drowned. You are a missing person, you know. Wasn't that a little careless? There were people who worried about you."

"I didn't think there would be anyone who would care." Thea made a small sound as if she had choked. "I didn't want to live with my aunt Josephine." He thought about saying "the Hawk" to get a reaction.

"Oh," Thea said simply. There was no indication, one way or the other, that she knew about his aunt Josephine. She washed the dishes, leaving them in the drain to dry. Cady sat where he was without offering to help. He watched her face, what he could see of it. He tried to read her thoughts. It made no sense the way this strange woman acted toward him. It made no sense that she didn't explain.

When she was through with the dishes, she said, "You must be tired." She motioned for him to follow her.

They went up the steep stairs from the kitchen. She opened the door at the top. Cady saw a little room, the ceiling slanting to four dormer windows across the end where he would have to sit on his knees to look out. The large bed filled most of the room. "Sleep well," she said. She paused at the door, studying him. Her eyes lifted from his feet to his jeans, too short, to his skinny arms, probably too long, Cady thought, and then directly into his eyes. A tremor twisted her mouth. Then she smiled, a remarkable smile, so much of it was in her eyes. She turned quickly and left the room.

3

When Cady awoke it was dawn. He lay on his arm and looked out the window. A pale lavender was creeping up from the edge of the pines. In the distance the fog cut off the rest of the world. Somewhere a single rooster crowed. Cady dozed off again and thought he heard Jenny cry. He longed for her to crawl in beside him. When he awoke the second time, a dazzling light was pouring in through the windows. He had not taken off his clothes. He must have slept as soon as Thea had closed the door.

He glanced up at the wooden bedposts, half as high as the ceiling. Directly across from him was an old oak chest. The sun caught it like a mirror. Cady was startled to find himself staring into two pairs of eyes above the chest. One of the dormer shutters was swinging open, splintering the light a hundred ways, giving life and substance to the faces of an old man and an old woman looking at him out of a huge frame. "Oh man!" Cady ducked his head under the covers.

23

Then he laughed at himself. He looked at the old couple again. The woman was small, her straight red hair drawn back into a knot. There was a sorrowful droop to her eye, and her lips did not smile. The old man's face was fragile, his features finely chiseled. His eyes were laughing out at Cady. He had a neat little mustache that followed his lips ever so closely. "If you want to watch everything I do from now on, okay. See if I care," Cady said out loud. After that he considered the room to be occupied by three persons, and he was never quite alone.

He heard a noise outside while he was changing his clothes. He looked out the window to see Thea running like a wild creature out of the pines at the back. Her hair was wet, lying flat to her head. She had on an old flannel robe that flapped at her heels. She seemed to be laughing and breathless. When she looked up toward his window, he stepped back out of sight.

Cady was in the kitchen when she came in. She brushed by him without a word. In a few minutes she returned dressed in jeans and a sweater. She had twisted her hair into a bun on the back of her head. She was bony and leggy, and looked like a boy to Cady.

"Good morning," she said. She had resumed her role of yesterday, quiet and reserved with him, except for her eyes—they were slightly out of focus, teary. "Our plumbing isn't too great. The shower needs fixing," she said. Then quickly, "Good morning, Mr. Myerling." She bit her lip. Her eyes moved across him in waves, as if not sure where to stop.

Cady was mad. He tried to hide it. "You made a mistake. I'm Cady Nicholson," he said.

24

She boiled water and stirred in oatmeal, and made coffee. She put bowls and spoons and cream and sugar on the table. She slapped things down hard. She didn't talk. Cady felt himself freezing up on the inside.

She turned to him suddenly. "I was wrong, at least for now. I'll call you just plain Cady," she said. "We don't have to decide about the other name just yet."

He nodded, but she had made him feel as though he had committed a crime by insisting on his own name.

Thea looked out the window. "When you saw me this morning I was coming back from bathing," she said. "In the pond back of the pines. It's the only place for now, unless you take a spit bath. I'll show you sometime. We don't have a tub." She shrugged. "But I don't mind. I find it quite invigorating. Of course, next winter we'll have to do something different if we can't fix it—maybe have a hot tub in the middle of the kitchen floor."

"Maybe I won't be here next winter."

"Maybe you will."

Cady ducked his head, then raised it again and looked her in the eyes. Her gaze was as direct as an arrow.

During the rest of the morning he tried to stay out of her way. He sat on the back porch for a while, swatting flies on the screen door and watching the crazy antics of the befuddled chickens. He counted how many times the silliest one, the only white chicken in the pen, ran for feed that one of the others got to first. He walked down and looked in the barn that was empty as a haunted house, save for an old car. Except for the chickens that roosted in the corner over the stalls, all that was left of the animals were

25

smells, and some hay in the mow. After lunch he helped clear the table, and since Thea seemed to be in an awful hurry, he offered to do the dishes. A few minutes later, when he was sitting in the swing on the front porch, he heard the sputtering of the old car. He peeked around the house just in time to see Thea driving down the lane past the barn.

"Where are you going?" he called to her.

She waved from the old Plymouth. "I'll be back," she yelled. But she didn't stop.

He went upstairs, took his clothes out of Marrietta's old suitcase and hung them carefully in the closet outside his bedroom door. Now that he was alone he walked from room to room, searching through the house, trying to get the feel of things. He caught himself listening to the sounds of the house—the creaking of the steps, the bushes rubbing against the front window, the popping in the walls. The house smelled of wood smoke, and bread baking, and Johnson's wax. Cady ran from room to room now. He wanted to see deeper than the walls. He was looking for something intangible, something that would rise up and claim him, a sense of belonging here. He could never tie himself to people. It didn't last. People change. With people he was always alone, except when he lived with Marrietta and Jenny.

He went back into the front room and sat in the big rocker. He looked around at the old-fashioned secretary in the corner, and the huge davenport with its high back. The long table in front of the windows was piled with sheets of paper, a typewriter, a dictionary and a lamp. So far there was nothing that he had learned about Thea that she hadn't told him. His eyes settled on the brick fireplace. It looked used, and beside it was a large wooden crate filled with firewood, packed as neat as matchsticks. Cady began to lay a fire. First he put on some of the small wood, crisscrossing it to leave space for the air to flow through. Then he added the small logs, cut no longer than the span of his hand and about as thick as his wrist. If it was cool he would ask to light it tonight. He sat cross-legged in front of it for a long time, daydreaming. He saw the sprouting flame, the light shutting out the shadows, bringing Jenny and Marrietta closer to him.

When Thea hadn't returned by midafternoon, Cady started down the lane in the direction she had gone. Through a clump of pines he saw the sparkle of water, the pond that Thea had told him about. He took off running through the woods. It was more like a small lake, longer than it was wide, and purple, almost black, in the depths. Reflected clouds floated across the water.

Cady took off his clothes and waded into the chill water. He saw the flat stones on the bottom, and his feet looked like white fish among them. Somewhere he could hear water running. He went in up to his waist. He leaped and squatted and splashed. Once in a while he sat still, and his eyes followed to the end of the pond where the stream must feed it. He searched the trees to see if anyone was around. He scrubbed himself with his hands, rubbing his legs and arms and chest.

Accustomed to the temperature now, he stooped down, leaving only his head above the water. There was no current. The water moved quietly past his chin. He closed his eyes. He forgot the mysterious Thea.

Then without warning he stepped into a hole, and

his head went under. It was like a nightmare. All the terrible memories of the flooded creek hit him for the first time, the swiftness of the current and the feeling of drowning. He remembered how he had been rolled and tossed, his head submerged part of the time, the voice of someone calling to him as he was swept away—and the roaring water became the Hawk screaming at him. The terror of that day long ago made Cady weak. It was as real as though it had just happened.

He splashed to his feet and ran from the pond. He was shaking as much from shock as cold. He rubbed himself with his shirt to stop shivering. Cady thought of how he had saved himself, treading water and being washed into the half-submerged tree. As he shuddered at the memory, he felt the relief of never having to go back home to the Hawk.

After he was dressed, he found the path to Thea's house.

4

It was almost dark when Thea came home. She had bought two boxes of groceries, a pair of jeans for Cady and a dozen packages of seeds and onion sets. He helped her carry the boxes in. Earlier he had started a fire in the kitchen stove, and the teakettle was steaming. In the corner of the cupboard he had found a huge blue teapot, shaped like Aladdin's lamp.

Thea looked at him as she had the first time, like she was startled to see him there.

"I'm glad you didn't run off," she said.

"Did you think I would? I would tell you first. You didn't tell me ahead you were going anywhere."

"I went without telling you because I couldn't take you with me." She held up the jeans to Cady. "Do you know why?"

"Why?"

"Because we have to come to an agreement about your name. You know you can't go by more than one name. And that's all each one of us has, is one name, and yours is Cady Myerling."

He tried to look her in the eyes without blinking his, or giving any indication of backing down. She was much taller than he was, narrow and straight.

"Next time maybe you can go with me—when you learn your name." She gave him a quick look with eyes as unblinking as his were. She laid a chocolate bar down on the table in front of him.

Cady looked down at the candy bar. He didn't want to argue about his name. "Is that all you did, get groceries?"

"I had errands to run." Her voice sounded tired.

"While you were gone I took a bath at the pond."

"It's deep in the far end, so be careful, Cady."

Cady helped put the groceries away. When he had finished she cut the bread, and while the eggs were frying she made tea. When they sat across from each other, she said, "I'm glad you didn't leave."

"Did you expect me to?"

"No, but sometimes it's hard to know."

"Because I'm a stranger to you?"

"You're not so strange. You're just a common, ordinary boy." She smiled at him over her teacup.

"If I stay I could get a job," Cady said.

"You don't need a job. You will go to school."

"Just maybe."

"Now you're talking nonsense." She pointed to his candy bar. "Eat it." She laughed. Cady smiled back at her.

Later that night it started to rain, not heavy, but coming in gusts, as if someone were spraying with a hose. Cady lit his fire. Thea popped corn and poured melted butter over it. They sat cross-legged in front of the fire with only the flame for light.

"There is something that we have to get settled before you can go to school." Thea wiped her hands on a dish towel in her lap and handed it to Cady. "I hate to harp on it, but your legal name is Cady Myerling, and you must use it living here."

"That's not *your* name."

She hesitated. "True."

"Why should I, then? I have never been called by that name."

"You've been using your mother's name. Didn't you think about that?"

"It was old Gran's name, too."

"But it's not your father's name!" Thea jumped up and took the empty bowl to the kitchen.

"How do you know that?" Cady yelled after her.

It was minutes before Thea brought another bowl of popcorn and put it in Cady's lap. She did not answer his question. "I like the name Cady. It was the name your mother wanted, so your father named you Cady."

Cady felt a quickening, a warmth spread through his body. He had never heard anyone mention his father and mother together in this way. In the half-light he watched Thea, her thin face and her delicate brow, and her red hair that looked almost black tonight. She knew a lot of things about him.

"But I never heard the name Myerling before, if it is my name."

Thea looked surprised. She leaned forward, searching his face. "You've not heard that name before?" She touched his hand. She was unbelieving.

Cady shook his head. He thought for a moment.

31

He wasn't sure. It was like the memory of a tune, heard faintly, then it was lost, something he couldn't recall.

Thea sat for a long time, quiet, her chin in her hand, staring into the fire. Then she said simply, "Your mother is dead." She paused. "And your father—what have they told you of your father?"

At first Cady didn't answer, but she waited.

"Nothing much. Different things." Cady flushed. It made his head hurt to think about it. He could hear the Hawk: "He ran out on you. He's probably dead." Cady's lips felt wooden. "My aunt Josephine never mentioned his name. She said he's probably dead."

" 'Nothing much,' " Thea repeated. "He's dead?" Her eyes narrowed. She looked away from Cady. "Did Marrietta say anything?"

Cady shook his head. "She was always frightened when I asked questions. Do you come from Spencer's Grove, too, where old Gran and Marrietta lived?"

"Not far from there." She carefully wiped the butter and salt off her hands.

Cady felt Thea drawing away from him. Her openness was gone. "I lived with Marrietta when I was a little kid, out in the country somewhere," he said. He waited a moment before he asked, "Did you know me then?"

"I knew of you, but I wasn't around there, then." Her face was closed. She was looking away from him. It made him angry at her secretive ways. He felt like shouting at her. Instead, he said, "What if I won't change my name?"

"You will." Thea's voice was tight and controlled.

Later, as Cady was crawling into bed, he heard her

come partway up the stairs. "Are you awake?" she called. He didn't answer. "I just want you to know I was glad to find you here when I got home, without having to tie you to the bed." She waited again for him to answer. He didn't. "You stayed. . . . I was afraid you wouldn't." Her voice was soft. He didn't think she intended him to hear that.

He was almost asleep when he heard her come into his room later. He lay still, his eyes closed. She stood beside his bed quietly. He wondered what her face would tell him. Was she glad that he was here? Would she look pleased or angry? And why did she stand and look at him? It was minutes before she left.

The rest of the night Cady's sleep was uneasy. He woke early when he heard Thea moving around in the kitchen. She was mixing a huge pan of bread dough when he came downstairs. She dumped it out on a board and began to knead it. Her arms seemed awfully small around and not strong enough. When Cady leaned against the counter watching her, she broke off a piece and pushed it across to him, and without saying a word showed him how to work the dough. He watched her for a few minutes, then began pulling at the dough and flopping it back over on itself. It stretched like a piece of rubber. They worked side by side for several minutes.

"I hope you washed your hands good," she said.

"I've sure got them clean now, if they weren't." He smacked the dough hard, rolled it into a ball and put it in the pan she gave him. Thea laughed at the funny-looking loaf, but said nothing.

After they had eaten breakfast, Cady was given the job of feeding the chickens and gathering the eggs.

The crazy white chicken followed him around the barn, and he shooed the other chickens away so she could eat. When he came back in the house, Thea was at her typewriter, not willing to talk. It was a relief when later in the afternoon Thea called him to the kitchen. She took two packages of meat out of the refrigerator, and wrapped a loaf of fresh bread and put it all in a sack.

"I want you to deliver these for me," she said. "When I go to the store I buy meat and groceries for Ingvald Peterson. He farms my land so I'm able to live here. He's an old neighbor down the road, a friend." She put the sack in Cady's arms. "He knows about you." She said the words quickly.

"What's there to know about me?"

"Your name." Thea gave a nod. "I wanted you to be prepared." She pointed out the kitchen door. "Take the back lane out to the road, turn right and he is about a half mile. It's the only house you'll see."

The lane was narrow and full of holes, with trees meeting overhead. The road he turned off on was not much better, but there were no trees, nothing but an ocean of wheat rippling in the path of the wind. It grew to the edge of the road, with no fences. Ingvald's house was easy to find. It was painted brick red, two stories with a green roof, and there were eight goats in the fenced-in front yard and a windbreak of pines to the north of the house.

By the time Cady reached the door with a billy goat at his heels, Ingvald stood waiting for him. He shoved the goats away from the door and motioned Cady inside. He was short and heavy and he had a deep hearty laugh. "You must be Cady Myerling," he said.

Cady flinched. He was never going to get used to that name. Every time he heard it, it made him nervous and gave him an upset stomach. He wondered what else this stranger knew. If he knew the name Myerling, did Ingvald know his father? Cady felt his cheeks burning. Did he have the same low opinion of his father that the Hawk did? Cady wished he could vanish into the woodwork—disappear completely. Maybe that was what he was supposed to do, and let Cady Myerling take over. But he wasn't ready to do that.

He shifted uncomfortably. He looked at Ingvald again to see if he was possibly reading his thoughts. Ingvald was in his sixties, his face as pink as a summer sunset. He had white hair to his ears and a boxer's nose, and his speech was as rich and thick as cream. And he was a good talker, Cady learned. Without giving Cady a chance to refuse, he poured him a cup of strong coffee. Cady took a gulp. The kitchen was cluttered with a couch, a table and an easy chair. There was a strong cheesy smell in the house. When Cady was given a slice of Thea's bread and a piece of cheese, he wrapped the whole slice around it.

"Goat's cheese," Ingvald said. Cady tried to swallow a whole bite without chewing. Ingvald sat down across the table from Cady. He smiled at him. "I think this is going to work out fine." He didn't explain what he meant. He spent thirty minutes telling Cady about the quail, the deer and the gray wolves and fox that crept to the edge of his trees. While he talked, he picked up a block of wood.

Cady watched the old man's hands as they began carving. Ingvald looked up and smiled. "An old man must keep in touch with his soul, so he tries to make something beautiful." He reached into a drawer for another knife. "And that's where it starts, right in a man's soul, and it works itself out to his hands." He laughed quietly. "What goes into my mind and my heart comes out here." He tapped the piece of wood he was carving.

The old man's hands were thick and scarred, and his fingers stubby, but the piece he was carving was delicate and alive. It was a bird with outspread wings.

"I should be going," Cady said, but he lingered. He told Ingvald about Thea's crazy white chicken that didn't have enough sense to find her food, and about learning to work the bread dough into a loaf. Ingvald could listen as well as talk. Cady began to relax. He thought even his bones felt soft. He was so comfortable, he couldn't resist saying, "Thea said you know about me."

Ingvald adjusted his thick glasses, blinking his eyes several times. "What should I know?"

Cady shrugged.

"I see a red-headed boy across from me. He appears to be a mighty fine boy—pretty much like Thea told me." His eyes were so friendly that Cady knew he could believe him. Ingvald took the sack that Cady had brought the meat and bread in, laid the bird carving in it carefully and folded the top closed. "This is for you."

On the way home Cady tried to imagine exactly where a man's soul was. Probably in the very center of his body, somewhere near his heart, and he saw it like an X ray, a transparent mass, working its way down his arms into his hands. It made Cady smile.

36

5

It took Cady three days with Thea's help to get the garden plowed. The fourth day they planted the seeds. Thea blocked out the garden like piecing a quilt. She walked back and forth, her hands clasped in front of her. "We'll put tomatoes down in that corner, the peas here and the corn over there along the side."

"And hide the watermelon between the rows," Cady added.

They set the onions, a hundred of them. Thea worked on her knees in the dirt, her hair hidden under an old bandanna. She was mud up to her elbows. "My mother always canned green beans—I think as many as a hundred quarts." Thea suddenly looked up. Her face was thoughtful. "Do you know, Cady, I have the strangest feeling, as though all this has happened before. You know, like—on a clear day you can see forever—forward and backward." Thea shivered, then she sighed. "My dad always put in a garden at home. We all worked in the garden together." She paused.

"My brother, too. That's what I remember." She thought for a moment. "It's queer, isn't it, how things connect in your mind."

"Why? What's there to connect—because I'm helping you make the garden?"

Her eyes rested on him. "I guess because I'm not alone now." She sat back on her heels, studying Cady. She rubbed a dirty hand across her face. "No, you're right. What's there to connect? It couldn't have been you. Oh, everyone has these crazy sensations they want to believe. It's like horoscopes. They're fun, but not necessarily true." When Cady didn't answer, Thea dropped to her knees and started working again. She looked up at him from time to time. "What are you thinking, Cady? You look so serious."

"I was wondering about your folks. Where are they now?"

"They're dead. They died a year apart. They lived near Spencer's Grove. They moved there before I was born."

"Where I lived with old Gran?"

Thea nodded.

"How about your brother?" Cady hobbled along in a squatting position, keeping up with Thea as she worked.

"Why don't you get busy and plant some seeds?" Thea tore the top off a package of peas and shook them into her hand. "Take the rest and plant them— straight rows." She worked without talking. When she had finished the row, she said, "My brother has his own way of doing things."

The wind quickened, as it does before a storm. It

brought with it the strong flavor of the earth and its greenness. They worked fast trying to beat the storm, but the rain soaked them before they got back to the house.

It didn't stop for two days, and most of the time it was foggy in the morning and evening, as if the world were submerged at the bottom of the sea. Cady went from window to window until Thea suggested he could do the dishes and pick up the house while she typed.

He noticed a wet spot shaped like a poodle in the middle of his bedroom ceiling. In the afternoon on the second day when the sun came out, he decided to crawl up on the roof and try to patch it. He found a bundle of shingles and some rusty nails in the barn.

Thea had left at noon in the car without saying where she was going again. He heard her yelling at him as soon as she spotted him from the drive when she drove in that evening.

"Get down from that roof! What if you fall? You could break your neck!" She stood below him, waving her arms. But she seemed extra cheerful to Cady when they went into the house, each carrying a sack of groceries. She pulled her hair back in a rubber band, put a dishtowel around Cady's waist, and asked him to pick over the box of strawberries on the counter while she made shortcake. While the cake was baking she fixed hamburgers and sliced a bowl of onions.

They were eating their shortcake when she said, "Cady, you've got to have more fun. I don't mean to work you to death. You don't need to stay so close around the house. We've got lots of woods around here. Why don't you do some exploring? Go see what you can find. If you go off toward the road, there's a creek down there, and good fishing. And you know about the pond."

She puzzled Cady. She seemed to be pushing him to go. He had thought she hadn't wanted him to leave the house, at least not to go far. But the next afternoon she packed him a lunch and waved him good-bye. That first day he didn't go far, only to the pond, where he ate lunch and looked for crawfish in the rocks around the water. Almost every day after that, if it was hot, Thea packed him sandwiches, and he headed for the woods where it was cool. Sometimes he swam in the pond. But he started going farther, making his own trails, marking the trees with a hatchet Thea had given him.

In the next week he found places where it seemed no one had been, back in the tangled thickets that he had to chop out as he went, where the mosquitos and gnats chewed at his ankles. One day he was working his way on the far side of the pond where he had seen ledges climbing steeply upward. He stumbled head-first through the bushes and landed at an opening in the rocks. It led into a cave hidden by overhanging rocks. He had to cut out a small pine to make it easier to crawl into the cave. He felt his way on his knees. After a few feet there was no light from the opening. He held his arms out to either side. He touched all around. There was barely room to move. He was ready to back out when suddenly he felt space around him. Cady put out his arms and slowly stood up. He walked a few feet forward until he touched a wall. He counted the steps. Then he walked to the side and

40

counted the steps. Walking completely around the square of the cave, he felt his way. The walls were dry and fairly smooth.

Cady laughed out loud. It sounded silly to him, laughing all by himself in a dark cave. "This is mine. I found it. No one can find it but me!" He said it quite loudly, and this caused him to laugh harder. When he left for home Cady threw the pine tree across the mouth of the cave. He looked back several times to be sure he could find it again.

"You've been gone for hours." Thea was slicing onions into a skillet of zucchini. Without looking up, she said, "I thought you weren't coming back." She laughed like it was a joke, but Cady knew it wasn't. She was always nervous when he had been gone a longer time than usual. She wiped at her eyes with the back of her hand. Her nose sounded plugged. "Onions," she said.

He set the table and poured the milk. Suddenly he decided not to tell Thea about the cave. It was something he would like to belong just to him. He felt her eyes on him, watching everything he did. He would keep it a secret.

"What's on your mind?" It seemed Thea always wanted to know what was on his mind, especially when he came back from the woods.

"It's private . . ." he began. At the look on Thea's face, he said, "I mean, I would like to keep it secret, something for myself—something I found today."

"What did you find today?" She wiped her hands on a towel and sat down at the table.

"Nothing much. Just a cave," he said.

He was relieved that she didn't ask too many questions about the location. All he told her was that it was in the cliffs beyond the pond.

"Oh, that's something I didn't know about," she said.

"I thought I might stay overnight sometime."

"That's your right, I guess." She went back to the stove and stirred the zucchini. "Snakes?"

Cady shuddered and thought of crawling on his knees into the cave, and running his hands around the walls. "I didn't see any. I'll take a flashlight next time." He was glad to see the interest in her face. "I think I'd like to fix it up, just for my own."

"Someplace to go to be alone, in other words." She paused. "Nobody else?"

"That's important to me. Something that belongs to me."

"I think I know what you mean." She smiled at him, then she laughed. It sounded to Cady like a bell had dropped and rolled across the floor.

"Something that nobody can take away from me."

"Okay. No interference, I promise."

The next afternoon Cady examined every corner of the cave with a flashlight, looking for snakes. He cleaned the flat ledge that ran across the back of the cave, and covered it with an old oilcloth Thea gave him. Next he brought in a pail filled with pine needles which he dumped onto the cave floor, making a thick carpet. Thea found a plastic cup and plate for him, and she dug an old quilt out of the attic. He kept it folded tight in a plastic bag, and put it up high in a hollowed-out place in the rock. Finally he brought magazines, matches, and a candle in a coffee can. When he mentioned to Thea that he was going to cut wood and pile it at the mouth of the cave, she warned him of the bitter weather to come in the winter, and not to be fooled. "When it is dry and cold a man can freeze to death before he knows it," she said.

On the first rainy day he built a fire at the entrance to the cave. He lay on his stomach and watched the fire, his eyes following the flame up until it turned to smoke and then drifted away. Cady drifted, too, quiet and full of dreams. He wondered if this was the peaceful feeling that most people had, especially those who belonged somewhere. But intruding upon Cady's dreams was Thea. He imagined he could see her face in the flames, strong and silent, telling him nothing. It had been over a month, and she had never explained more than being a friend of the family. He felt a rush of anger toward her. She wasn't being fair.

One night, after two weeks of Cady barely making it home on time for supper, Thea was sitting on the back steps waiting for him. She watched as he came up through the backyard. "I hardly see you anymore," she snapped. "I didn't intend for you to move out there."

Cady ducked his head. "I'm sorry."

"What on earth do you do? Do you spend all your time in the cave? Davy Crockett living alone in the wilds?"

"Something like that."

"Your supper is on the table getting cold." She got up and marched into the kitchen ahead of him. While he ate, she sat across from him, watching him, hardly eating herself.

Cady soaked his bread in his bean soup. He didn't

want to explain to her how he felt about the cave, that it was his act of possession, something that couldn't disappear overnight. It belonged to him, cut into the earth, rock solid. "I told you I like something belonging to me," he said. "People change. Places don't."

Thea poured them each a cup of tea. She shoved one across the table to Cady. "People don't always change. And did you ever stop to think you can love a place, but it can't love you back?"

"I like belonging somewhere." He shot her a dark look. "And knowing who I am, and not playing a lot of crazy games." He felt his face grow hot.

"But you do belong—and you are someone. You are Cady Myerling!" Her face was as flushed as his was.

Cady's fist hit the table with a crack. They glared at each other, their jaws set. They hadn't argued about his name for days. She kept trying to push that name off on him. A name that belonged to someone who had run away and left him—someone he didn't know.

But after that Cady stayed home from the cave. He was ashamed of storming at Thea the way he had. Her anger toward him had frightened him. She had been so quiet since. Cady tried to make up for it. He suggested that he put up a new fence for the chickens to run in. Thea had to go into town to get the lumber and fencing. She didn't ask Cady to go with her. Instead, she dropped him off at Ingvald's. She said she would stop later to pick him up, and not to forget the milk and cheese that Ingvald made for her. "Help Ingvald," she said, as she drove off.

The old man was emptying the small room at the back of the house. It had been used as a storeroom

44

for a dozen boxes of junk, old dishes, jars and empty coffee cans. Cady helped him pull some of the larger boxes out to the yard. In two of them were blankets that he hung on the line.

"I think maybe I'm going to have company," Ingvald said.

Cady followed him back to the little room. Ingvald started wiping down the walls. He breathed so hard he sounded as if he were going to burst. The sweat ran down like tears on his cheeks. Cady took the old towel from him and did the rest.

"Who?" he finally asked.

"This boy—you might like him. It'd be good if you did."

Cady waited for him to continue, while the man poured them each a glass of milk and cut them hunks of cheese.

"He's my niece's boy. He's a little slow, and he's had a bad time. He's hard to handle—so his mama says. She's got two others and no papa now."

Ingvald bit off the cheese and chewed on it for a minute. Cady noticed his teeth had spaces between them, and his face had so many crisscrossing lines that it was hard to tell if he was happy or sad. Ingvald got up and went to the door of the small room. "I'm aiming to put a bed in there and some curtains. Do you think it will look all right?"

"Not bad. When is he coming?"

"I don't know for sure. He isn't exactly agreeable to it."

Cady studied Ingvald's face again. "You worried?"

"Some. I want him to make up his own mind. I don't like dragging anyone here against their will."

Cady thought of Thea sending for him, a strange kid she didn't know. She must have worried, too. Maybe she still did. A shock ran up his arms and ended in his chest. He wondered what might happen because he hadn't given in about changing his name.

By the time Thea came, the sun had escaped behind the trees and was sending lacy patterns across the road. But she came from the direction of their land, not town. Cady wondered why she had gone home alone first.

He began going into the woods again at Thea's urging, but he was careful to come home early. The first time he saw the strange man was the day that instead of going straight to his cave, Cady had circled around through the pines and climbed up the cliff behind it. Here the brush was wild and thick, sometimes towering over his head. Before he realized it, he had climbed to the top of the cliff. Standing close to the edge, he balanced himself, leaning against a huge jack pine, and tried to see his cave below. He was glad there was no sign of it.

Out of the corner of his eye he saw something move, a flash of copper or bronze—an animal, he thought. It was so quick it might have been the sun momentarily reflecting on metal. Then a whistle, hardly audible to Cady. He turned full face to see where the sound came from. A man stepped out of the shadows of a grove of trees farther down the cliff. He seemed part of the forest. His clothes were green, and speckled with light and shadow. A disguise almost, except for the hair that was bright as a torch, catching Cady's eye.

Cady moved carefully so as not to attract the man's attention. But he hadn't taken two steps when the man had disappeared. Cady ran in the direction he had seen the man, but he was gone, leaving no sign, as if he had never been there.

The silence wrapped around Cady. It was frightening. The man had been like a vision. Cady took a deep breath. Maybe it was his imagination—maybe he would see a man behind every tree. But the woods seemed so empty now, and Thea had never mentioned anyone living so nearby.

Cady went down to his cave, but he didn't stay long. On the way home he watched out for the man. For reasons he didn't understand, except that he didn't want his trips to the cave stopped, Cady decided not to tell Thea about the man.

"What about school this fall?" Thea asked at breakfast the next day.

It was a hot July morning. They went out to sit on the back porch steps to finish their coffee. The air was soggy. Everything drooped. The grapevines dragged on the ground and the hibiscus had collapsed.

"Do you want to go?" she asked.

"If you want me to, I suppose I'd better."

Her quick smile came; then her face turned serious. "I think you should go to school. There's not much choice in what you do with your life without school."

"I won't argue."

"But that isn't enough. You must want to go for your own sake—not mine."

Cady shrugged.

"I suppose you've some catching up to do."

"Lots. I lost more than a year."

Starting that night, as soon as the table was cleared from supper, Thea brought out a box of books, paper and pencils. She piled the social studies, math and history books on one corner of the table and sat down across from Cady. "Remember I was a teacher once," she said without a smile.

The first week Cady studied most of the day, and in the evenings Thea went over the work with him. The second week he tried to keep ahead of her. If he went to the cave he took a book with him, and he kept the history book under the bed and studied late into the night. Cady wanted to prove how smart he was to Thea.

He knew she was trying out some of her new math on him when she gave him problems. One night he worked a math problem faster than she did. He sat waiting for her to finish, a grin on his face.

The next night Thea tried one of her mindbogglers on him. "Would you please tell me," she said, "if a certain fish's tail weighs nine pounds, and its head weighs as much as the tail and one third of the body combined, and its body weighs three times as much as the tail, what does the fish weigh?"

Cady glanced once at her and once at the ceiling. "Fifty-four pounds," he snapped.

"You're really a showoff," she said, laughing.

Later, when he had finished working the problems

in his lesson, she said, "You're good at math." She sat back and looked at him. "Extra good—really quite brilliant." She thumbed through the book. "That's a year ahead of where you should be." Her face was amused, but there was also another expression. Cady thought it was pride.

When it was hot they talked long into the night. After the mosquitos quit biting, they went out on the back porch. Thea talked about the little bay city where she had lived. Cady urged her to tell him more. He listened closely, always hoping for a hint as to how she fit into his life.

"It was on the gulf," she said. "Not far from Corpus Christi. There was an old hotel, where I lived. It must have been close to a hundred years old, with colonnades and little tables out in front, with huge umbrellas. And down at the end of the walk a chinaberry tree filled with birds, and smelling like someone had spilled a bottle of perfume." Thea sat quietly, her eyes like two moons. "I wish you could have been there. You could watch the shrimp fleet coming in with the sea gulls circling."

A few days later Cady asked her to tell him more. It was after they had finished the lessons. She dished them out bowls of ice cream, and dribbled strawberry jam over it. They sat on the back steps. A slight breeze had come up. The moonlight flowed in between the trees like a river.

"Did you know I was married once?" Thea's voice came quick and light. When Cady shook his head, she said, "He was an officer at the Naval Air Station in Corpus Christi. I lived at Palacios, not far from there. We spent weekends together. We danced in a ballroom over the water, part of the pier. I wish you could have seen it." Cady noticed her ice cream was melting and nudged her. She spooned the soft ice cream and sipped it. "From the window in our room you could see the ocean, and at night before we went to bed we walked out on the pier and sat on the bench out on the end of it. We watched the moon roll in on the waves. Sometimes they hit tremendously hard, swaying the old pier like a boat." Thea sat with her eyes closed, rocking back and forth as if she were there.

The strange powers of Thea brought the sea to Cady. He felt the trembling of the pier against the waves.

"We were married for only three months," she said. She had a choppy way of talking now. "One day he flew out over the gulf, and he never came back. I was nineteen."

In the silence Cady felt her loss as if it was his own.

"A lot of people get left, you know," Thea said. "We have to adjust to disappointment, and we have to forgive, too, God, or whoever made it happen."

Cady looked into Thea's face. She must have gone a long time without talking to anyone about herself. But there was nothing he knew to say. He was only a young boy.

By the middle of August, the grass had turned brown and the leaves were curling from the heat. The ground was as hard as limestone. Cady usually took a dip in the pond before going on to his cave, the coolest place he could find. He had added some old pans, a wooden bench and a pillow that Thea was going to toss out. She had also given him a straw mat that he laid over the pine needles on the floor. He kept raisins in a coffee can, and a jar of peanuts Thea had brought him from town.

Thea had given him books, too, that she had found in the house when she moved there, some of them old and tattered. "Probably belonged to my grandparents," she said. He put the books in the plastic bag with the quilt. Most of them he had never heard of before. Booth Tarkington, Rudyard Kipling and Horatio Alger were the authors. It wasn't so much he wanted to read them, it was gathering things around him that were his.

Thea was gone from time to time, always alone, and Cady had never gone farther down the road than Ingvald's farm. One afternoon, when it cooled to below ninety degrees, Cady walked out to the jack pines that edged Thea's fields. The yellow stubble of wheat felt hot, and looked as though the sun had exploded in it. But a cooling wind came gusting through the trees.

It was in the trees that Cady saw the man again. He was hard to follow, as he had been the first day. He slipped from tree to tree, disappearing for seconds, then reappearing. He wore camouflage clothes and looked like a hunter, although he wasn't carrying a gun. A cap covered his hair, so he was harder to see this time. Cady paced himself, trying not to be impatient. He followed the man for almost a half mile. Just as Cady was wondering what he would say if he caught up with him, the man disappeared as quickly and completely as if he had never been in the woods with Cady. Cady started running; he even yelled. He searched for a long time before he went back to his cave. The only live thing that he saw was a red fox trotting across the stubble in the wheat field.

Cady was glad to crawl into the darkness of his cave. Staring out the opening, still watchful, he felt safe in that separate world where no one could see him. He tried to picture the strange man whose face he had never seen. He wasn't even sure of his size, whether he was large or small. The man didn't seem to be dangerous—he was going about his own business. It was Cady who was sneaking about, trying to discover another's secrets. The man's only crime was to be mysterious, as if he were playing a game. That's when Cady started thinking of it as a game, and when he decided again for sure that he would not betray the man to Thea or to anyone.

Cady had grown accustomed to the rustling of the wind in the leaves that sounded like rain. It had almost put him to sleep. He was trying to read when he heard a different sound. He saw a pair of legs, then someone squatting in the opening of the cave, staring in at him. It was a boy, homely as Cady had ever seen. His teeth were huge and pushed against his lips.

"I wondered where you were," the boy said matter-of-factly. He had a slight stutter.

Cady didn't speak. He had the crazy idea that by not speaking he would become invisible, and the face would go away.

"I followed you here. It wasn't hard." The boy said.

Cady slowly closed his book. "Who the heck do you think I am?"

"You're Cady Myerling, in case you don't know."

The use of that name startled Cady and made him want to slug the kid in the mouth. He eased himself out of the cave without appearing to give ground. The kid was even homelier seen up close. He had jug ears, and his eyes seemed as flat in expression as fried eggs.

"I think you have the wrong guy," Cady said. "And this cave belongs to me—so take the hint!"

"I don't like that kind of talk for no reason." The boy sat down on a stump in front of Cady. "But I figured it was your cave." Resting his chin on his fists, he said, "My uncle said to come and see you, else I wouldn't be here."

"Your uncle?"

"Uncle Ingvald, down the road. He told me to get

acquainted. That's why I'm here. I'm Pete." He spit between his feet. "And I ain't going to stay long."

"That's okay with me. Anyway, I knew you were coming to live with him. How long you staying?"

There was suddenly such dismay in the boy's face that Cady was sorry he had asked.

"Who knows?" Pete said. "As long as I can stand it, or he can stand me."

"Me, too—who knows?" Cady said. He felt better toward Pete.

"Are you going to go to school here?" Cady asked. Pete shrugged. "I probably can't get out of it."

"Me neither." The boys grinned at each other.

"You haven't been here so long yourself," Pete said with a sly look.

"Do you know anyone here?"

"Naw."

"Same here," said Cady. "Have you been here before? I mean, with your Uncle Ingvald?"

"Once."

"Ingvald said you weren't agreeable to coming."

Pete bristled. "What else did he say?"

"Not much. I was there when he was fixing you a room."

"Did he tell you why I'm here—because there ain't enough room at home for all of us, and I'm getting pushed out the door, and because my ma's mad at me? My sister will be next."

"What's her name?"

"Velda." He sounded more cheerful. "She's a lot like me, only she's smarter. She's a year older, too." He picked at the bark on the stump. His fingers were

55

stubby like Ingvald's. "I'm not going to stay any longer than I have to. I'm going home and get a job. Then Velda and me can live by ourselves."

Later Cady and Pete walked together until they reached the place in the drive where Pete had to turn off to go home. "See you around," Cady said. Then he thought of something. "When you were following me, did you see anyone else?"

Pete shook his head.

"Did you see a fox?"

"I've never seen a fox, and I'd run like heck if I did," Pete said.

8

A week before school started, Thea took Cady into town for the first time in her old Plymouth. He had hardly seen Moravia when he passed through on the bus. He hadn't missed much. The town had one department store, a tavern and a civic center in a renovated garage. Main Street was paved for three blocks, and the rest of it seemed made of dust that drifted in clouds over the houses set close to the road. Moravia was flat and lonely looking as far as Cady was concerned.

In the department store Thea nudged him in the back when she introduced him as Cady. No mention of his last name. "His mother has passed away," she said. "He has come to live with me." And no mention of how long ago, or any other particulars. She held up jeans to him that were inches big in the waist to get them long enough. She bought three pairs. The clerk, a very nice old lady, kind of thin and dried-up looking, said, "He should be wearing slims, but we don't have any. Do you think you can manage to keep these up, sonny?" She cocked her little head and looked at Cady like a bird at a worm. Cady's tongue felt wedged behind his teeth, making it hard for him to answer.

Instead of T-shirts, which he would have preferred, Thea bought him three long-sleeved shirts with sport collars. When he wrinkled his face, she laughed. "Give me time to get used to buying for a boy." She gave him a quick smile, mostly with her eyes. "Anyway, you don't have dress-up clothes. I think you should." She slipped her arm through his when they went out of the store.

Next they went to the grocery store. Thea had a long list of staples. Then she bought the usual groceries for Ingvald, mainly meat and potatoes and head lettuce. The last thing she decided on was a box of Mars bars.

After shopping they stopped at the tavern, which surprised Cady at first, but it seemed to be an afternoon social club. At the front were several ladies having sandwiches and coffee. The men sat separately, in the back, drinking beer. Thea and Cady picked a booth midway.

Thea suddenly slumped, her arms resting on the table as if they were too heavy. "Well, that's done," she said.

Cady wondered what she meant—buying his clothes, buying the groceries or bringing him to town with her. He had been hidden away and his name had been changed. He couldn't forget that. "It's all right for people to know about me now?" he asked.

"Yes. It took time." Her eyes didn't waver from

Cady's face. "I don't believe there will be any problems."

"What kind of problems?" A kernel of fear made Cady's hands clammy, and his breath come quickly.

Thea brushed her hair back impatiently. It was smooth and shiny like mahogany, and parted down the middle in exact line with her nose. Sometimes Cady thought an invisible line divided her down the middle into two people, one happy with him, the other nervous and afraid for him.

"Don't frown that way. It's no big deal," she said. "Forget it." Her fingers danced across the menu. "What will you have?"

They ordered hamburgers, Cokes and chocolate sundaes.

On the way home they drove out past the school Cady was going to attend. It sat in the middle of a wheat field, a long low building. One half of the grounds was blacktopped, and the other was a baseball diamond surrounded by grass.

On the Tuesday after Labor Day Thea stood over Cady at six o'clock in the morning. After calling gently in his ear, she put up the shades. At the door she gave him a thumbs-up sign. It was the first day of school. Cady had pains in his stomach. He was always having to start over again. He hated beginnings and endings.

When he went down to the kitchen in his new jeans, taken in at the waist, and a new shirt with a collar, Thea was at the stove stirring a pan of oatmeal. She filled a bowl for him, and handed him a pitcher full of cream thick enough to cut with a knife. Beside his plate Cady found a bundle of paper, two ballpoint pens, and five pencils.

Thea sat down across from him and sipped her coffee. "Do you think you are ready for school—Cady Myerling?"

Cady chose not to answer her.

She put her cup down carefully on the table. "You know it has to be that way—I mean your name. I registered you last week. I told them you had been out of school for quite a long time, and I had been teaching you. I gave them the grades I made out for you from the work you did for me. The principal is going to start you in eighth grade. Maybe you'll go on to ninth soon. You're smart." Suddenly Thea's voice changed. "You can't go by your mother's name!" She slapped her hand down on the table so hard the sugar bowl rattled. "You'll use your father's name."

She looked so funny that Cady laughed. Her face was almost as red as her hair, and in her anger her hair flew on either side of her head like the wings of a bird. She looked surprised for a minute. "I don't know why you're laughing," she said defensively.

"The way you look—when you're mad. You look like a bird, like a redheaded woodpecker."

"You don't look so hot yourself!" She rubbed her face nervously and some of her hair tumbled down over her brow. Suddenly she began to laugh. She shook her head as if trying to clear it. "You'd better eat up if you're going to make the school bus. It will stop at the end of our lane. Pete will be on it, too, remember. Look after him today."

"Yah, I think he'll need it. He's scared. He says they'll kick him out because he's so dumb."

"It's up to you then to encourage him."

Cady shoved his face close to Thea's. "I'll look after him *if* I go." Their eyes collided. "I'm dumb, too—I don't even know my own name."

She touched his hand. "Please do as I ask. Please trust me." Her voice was low, and her face looked deflated.

Cady knew it wasn't right or natural for Thea to be this humble. He couldn't stand her staring at him this way with such a look of disappointment. "I didn't say I wouldn't."

"It's settled then?" she asked. "Cady Myerling?" She spoke the name softly.

Cady heard her take a deep breath. He started eating. He nodded his head.

When he was going out the door, she called him back. "Wait." She put a brown sack in his hand. "Your lunch. They won't have the cafeteria open until tomorrow." She held on to him. "Don't talk about what happened before you came here." She looked embarrassed. Her face grew pink. "I wouldn't tell them where I came from if I were you. When people asked, I talked about Texas as if we both might have lived there." She flushed again. "That's what you should do."

"Do you want me to lie?"

"No . . ."

"Then what?"

"You'll learn. There is a way—if you are careful— to avoid lying."

"If I don't tell the truth, it will have to be a pack of lies."

"Not necessarily. It's *how* you tell the truth. There

61

is the whole world to talk about, from any point of view. Pick your own subject." She followed him to the door. "But you don't have to put yourself on the line and let people read you like a book." She walked out on the porch with him. "You'll find a way without lying," she called after him.

What she had told him was true. It was easy after that first day of school, which was the worst one. "Myerling, Cady," the teacher, Mr. Pomeray, called out in a booming voice. After a few days Cady answered, "Here," without having to think twice about his name, and if he felt the blood rushing to his face, he ducked his head.

Whenever Cady saw Pete he was as much alone as Cady was. They sat with each other on the bus, and sometimes they ate lunch together. Pete had been put in the sixth grade. He was a head taller than the other kids, who flowed past him like minnows. Pete told Cady that they treated him like he had just stepped off another planet—a contaminated one. Cady felt the same way. Thea said that was ridiculous. Cady had to learn how to interact with others. "To get acquainted, you have to talk," she said.

Sure enough, Cady found that when he talked it brought him a quick audience. He repeated the stories Thea had told him about the gulf. He was careful. He did not lie.

"The waves on some days are as pale as skimmed milk, then they rise like smoke, and they fill the air. Oh man! About a mile high," he said. "And when they drop back into the sea—it's enough to make the world collapse. And on other days the water is clear and smooth, and the waves come silently, over and over like a heartbeat, even and strong."

Sometimes the older boys ganged up on him, testing and tormenting him. Usually two of the oldest ones, Spiketooth and Rubbermouth, led the pack.

"Hey, Myerling, you're going to freeze up here in Minnesota. Did you bring your long underwear?" Spiketooth yelled.

"Sure." Cady shrugged. Then the other voices came pelting him with questions.

"What's so great about the ocean? It's just so much water."

Cady made swimming motions.

"We got lakes up here, plenty of water."

"Don't it ever snow in Texas?"

Cady thought for a minute. "Nope, not at Galveston. You can run right down and jump in the ocean all winter. Have you ever tried surfing?"

"Have you?" someone asked in return.

Cady changed the subject. "They've got yachts there, too."

"How about those awful hurricanes? They can kill you."

"How *about* those hurricanes. It blew so hard one time that it took all the cement pier up, and left it in piles along the beach. Everything, the dance hall, the restaurant, everything was wiped out!" Cady spoke eagerly.

"It sure don't do that here."

"You don't have the bay, either. With the big old moon on it, and a place way out on a wooden pier where you can sit and watch it for hours." Cady spoke with as much feeling as Thea had. He saw it as clearly as she had painted it. "And you sure can't go out and get yourself a bushel of oysters anywhere around here!"

"How come you're up here, then, if it's so great there. Where's your folks?" Cady was surrounded by curious faces.

"My mom's dead." Cady hesitated. It sounded cruel the way he said it, dismissing it lightly. But he had never known her. He heard the Hawk again, calling her Violet, a flower, something torn from the earth and already returned to the shadows on the night of Cady's birth. As for his father, he didn't answer.

"You gonna stay long?" Bart, a big kid, asked this. He was tall and fat, and he looked old enough to be out of school. Cady looked at him quickly to see if he really wanted to know, or if he was baiting him. His eyes were friendly.

"I really don't know," Cady said honestly.

9

Cady got off the school bus at his corner. Pete tapped on the window and waved to him. Sometimes Cady walked up the narrow lane, other times he cut diagonally through the thickest part of the trees. It had rained and cleared, and the sky was transparent. The air was like silk against his skin, with just enough breeze to bring down the leaves like falling sparrows. One caught in Cady's hair and hung there for a moment. The little creek, running bank-full through the woods, carried some of the leaves away.

Cady jumped across and walked along beside the creek. Instead of going straight home he wandered off in the direction of the fields, following the stream. He was back in the woods again, where the creek curved sharply between the jack pines, when he heard the sound of barking. At first Cady thought it was a dog. He moved carefully. He had never seen a dog in the woods. Cady heard it a second time before seeing it ahead, playing in the water. It splashed into the stream and grabbed a stick. The sun coming between the trees caught the animal's fur, turning it golden. As he watched, it whirled, its bushy tail straight out, dancing. A fox, dancing. It threw itself on the ground, crouched on its belly, its head resting on its forepaws. Then it leaped into the air, light and graceful as if swept by the wind. Cady didn't move for fear of disturbing it.

He heard a whistle then, and the small red fox rolled over and over, its feet in the air. Cady heard someone laugh, and a stick was thrown but there was no sign of who had thrown it. The fox caught it, tossed it into the air, and caught it again. The man stepped into view. He was laughing. He reached down and scratched the animal's belly. When he started off through the trees, the fox followed.

Cady followed, too, as closely as he could. Several times the fox stopped and cocked its head, but it didn't run or act frightened. The man seemed unaware of Cady, so Cady was able to follow them into the trees deeper than he had ever been. Although the brush was thick and the trees close together, Cady discovered a narrow path that had been worn from long use. Once he lost sight of the man, but quickly caught up with him by following the path.

At the edge of the jack pines, Cady came to an abrupt stop and dropped down quickly into the thicket. In the middle of a small clearing, tucked in among the giant trees, was a house. The walls were logs. On the side facing Cady was a huge stone chimney, with smoke coming out of it. Behind it, Cady saw the fence line that marked Thea's property, and the rough pasture and rolling hills beyond. There was no sign of either the man or the fox.

Cady waited for several minutes before starting back. The days were getting shorter—it was almost the first of November—and the sun had suddenly dropped behind the trees. He was already late getting home. As it grew darker, he had difficulty following the path.

But Cady was too excited to think beyond the idea that the man must live in the cabin, here on the land that belonged to Thea. He had no proof of this, but the man had led him to the cabin before disappearing with the fox.

Cady was surprised to see that Thea had started out the back way to meet him. When she saw him, she called to him from a distance. "Cady is that you?" She walked toward him. "Why don't you answer me?" In the dark it was hard for Cady to see her face until he was almost upon her. "I couldn't see who it was." She buttoned her jacket and put her hands in her pockets.

"Who else?"

"It's dark. I couldn't tell." She was angry. "I was worried. Is that surprising to you?" She walked on ahead. "You didn't come home from school."

Cady tried to pass it off with a shrug and a grin.

"You looked different coming through the trees. It was dark. I couldn't see," she said, almost apologetic now. "I had a little scare." She tried to laugh. "I thought you were someone else. I forget you can take care of yourself."

Cady told her he had followed the creek and forgotten about the time. He wondered why she should be so worried that he was someone else. She must know about the man and the log house on her property, and she hadn't mentioned them to him. Cady figured he didn't have to mention them to her.

When they got home Thea quickly set the table. Cady tried to help her, but she didn't let him, whirling around and doing everything herself. She gave him a bowl of soup, but didn't eat any herself. Cady was hungry, and he didn't want to talk, but his mind wasn't on his eating. Instead he thought of the fox leaping and playing with the man, then following him when he started off through the trees.

After supper, when Cady went to the front room to study, Thea followed him in. Instead of reading, as she usually did, she sat and stared at nothing. Cady felt the silence ticking away in his head until he thought he would explode. He let his books slip off his knees onto the floor with a crash. Thea sighed loudly enough for him to hear.

"If you're sorry you had me come here—just say so," Cady said.

Thea looked at him, startled.

"You don't act like it's much fun—like maybe I'm a burden."

He could tell that Thea was trying to hide any show of feelings that might tell him more than she intended. She waited a moment before answering. "That's foolish. I'm not sorry. Are you?"

"I don't do much that pleases you."

"Maybe I don't please you, either." Thea folded her hands tightly, one over the other. "It's been better for me lately. A lot better to have you here with me.

I was hoping it was better for you, too." She leaned her head back against the chair.

It was chilly, so Cady made a fire. He tried to read his social studies book. It was so quiet again in the room he couldn't think. He noticed the shadows on the ceiling made by the firelight. They moved in rhythm as the sea might, or the flight of a gull. He tried to remember how Thea had described it to him.

She broke in on his thoughts. "I'd like to know more what you're thinking. It's better to talk. When you meander around in the woods alone, I worry, and you never tell me anything. You're so secretive." She paused. "Don't you ever see anyone?" Thea watched him carefully.

The question came so suddenly it caught Cady off guard. He kept his head down so she couldn't see his face. "I saw a fox today. He seemed almost tame." Cady waited before he looked up at her. There was a stillness in her eyes, as clouded as the depth of the pond where nothing showed.

"That's strange," she said. "Don't you think so?" She sounded disturbed. Cady hadn't intended that. "You saw nothing else?" she asked.

"I told you before, only the birds, and sometimes I hear a deer crashing through the trees, and except for that, I'm alone. Pete came once." Rather than meet Thea's eyes, Cady jumped up and went to the window. He looked out at the moon, which seemed ten times larger than usual. "Was the moon like this at Palacios?" To ease his feelings about the lie, he tried to imagine the pier and the sea, and the moon turning the waves to gold. "I'd like to see that place sometime."

"What place?"

"Palacios."

"You can someday."

"With you?" Cady turned to face her.

"Probably, if you would like that."

"You're not kidding about the oysters as big as your fist?"

"Why would I kid? When the tide is out you can find them by the bushel. You just wade out under the pier." Thea smiled at last. "I like to go shelling, too—not in the bays, but along the shore away from town." She was talking along, easy now. "I like to look for sand dollars, and snail shells that look like huge eyes staring at you—and conchs are there by the hundreds. Quite often they're inhabited by small crabs—hermit crabs. The crab twists its body into the spiral of a conch, leaving only its claws outside as a tightly fitting door. You could pound it to pieces, and the crab wouldn't leave."

Cady sat down on the stool in front of her. He leaned forward, chin propped in his hands, seeing with Thea's eyes.

"They say you could force them out by taking the conch from the water and putting it in the sun. Then the crabs leave the shell." She shuddered. "I didn't have the heart."

"I wouldn't have the heart, either, to make them leave." Cady's voice was emphatic, his eyes intense.

"But it's interesting." She paused. "No matter what the shape of the shell, the crabs manage to fit themselves to their homes. They adapt." Thea's eyes lingered on his face, meeting his briefly.

70

"You mean if they are going to stay, they'd better fit in."

"Oh, I wouldn't say that exactly. I mean the shells have all kinds of shapes, and still they suit hermit crabs for homes."

"So I'm a crab?"

Thea smiled first, then laughed out loud. She jumped to her feet, and took Cady by the hands and pulled him up with her. "I'm glad that you're here with me. I wouldn't have it any other way—remember that! We'll fight sometimes. You'll be sassy and I'll nag, but I'm not sorry. I get lonely for things the way they used to be—for family. So don't ask if I'm sorry. I'm not! It's better for both of us."

"But we're not really family."

"If we're not, we're good substitutes, aren't we?" She smiled wryly.

Before he went to sleep, Cady rolled up in his blanket, pulling it tight around him, from his neck to his feet, like a cocoon—no, better yet, like a conch shell.

10

On the next Saturday afternoon Cady went to his cave. It was a cool, gray day, so he built a fire. He lay beside it and tried to read. He looked up when he heard a noise. Pete was sitting on the stump, watching him.

When he saw Cady look up, Pete said, "Miss McVey told me to come and find you."

"She's a Mrs., and call her Thea. I do."

"I'm not supposed to. My uncle said so."

"That's okay."

"My uncle told me to get outside and get the stink blown off."

"How are you two getting along?"

Pete shrugged. "It could be better—it could be worse, and it ain't any worse than at home."

"Do you like school any better?"

"I never liked any school. I'm not so smart, you know. Uncle Ingvald makes me study, then he tries to help me. He does it all wrong."

"I could help you," Cady offered.

Pete got a shy grin on his face. "That'd be good."

"Is Ingvald a good cook? You look like you're getting fat."

"He can sure make good pancakes. We eat a lot of them. I get to run the churn for butter—that I hate." Pete was more talkative than usual. Sometimes coming home on the bus with Cady he wouldn't say a word.

"Do you know what I hate?" asked Cady. "Killing a chicken." He jumped to his feet and came around in front of Pete. "Do you know how the old Hawk kills chickens? She takes them by the head and swings them around and around like a pitcher winding up for a fast ball." Cady demonstrated. "She's got this look like she is just going to croak with joy. Her tongue sticks out between her teeth, and her eyes almost pop out of her head. She always looked worse than the dead chicken when she got through." Cady stuck out his tongue, and popped his eyes. "She looked like a chicken hawk." He stopped suddenly. "Anyway, she's mean. She's my aunt. I ran away from her." The words slipped out so easily Cady was frightened, but it didn't prevent the satisfaction he felt. "That's personal. I don't like to talk about it."

"Me either. I don't like to talk about things that make me mad." Pete nodded his head. There was respect in his eyes. "That makes us even, don't it?" His thick fingers twisted at a branch. He peeled back the outer layer, throwing it into the fire. "You ain't ever going back, then?"

Cady shook his head.

73

"I probably won't, either."

"I've been lots of places." Cady hoped it didn't sound like bragging.

"You like any of them?"

"Not especially—except the last one—my cousin's. I hated some of the places I lived."

"Then we'll probably stick around here for a while," Pete said. He pressed on his big front teeth, thinking. "Where'd you come from?"

Cady rolled his eyes and pointed south.

Pete grinned at him. "Okay, if that's the way you feel. Don't you ever get lonely for . . . " He pointed south, too.

"Not really."

"Don't you miss your family?" Pete was like a woodpecker, tapping away with his questions.

"I don't have anyone to miss."

Pete looked at him, puzzled. "Everybody dead, huh?"

"I guess you could say so."

"I miss my sister Velda. Ma is so taken up with DeDe, the baby. He doesn't look like me. Velda does. . . . I don't think Uncle Ingvald would want Velda—both of us."

"Did you ask him?"

Pete shook his head. "He's kind of grouchy with just me. He worries all the time. He thinks I did some real weird things before I came."

"Did you?"

"I smoked pot once." Pete pointed his finger at Cady. "Just once, and Ma used a belt on me. I said don't do that again, I'm warning you. And I shoplifted once and got caught. Ma said it was things like that that made my dad go away, so everything was left to her. We started fighting all the time, and I quit school for a while. She says no woman could handle me. That's why I'm here."

Cady was watching with fascination the saliva that bubbled at the corners of Pete's mouth when he got excited.

Then, quickly, Pete changed the subject. "Uncle Ingvald wants me to learn to make cheese." He made a face and groaned. "Did you ever notice how his house smells? He's got bags of curds hanging all over the kitchen getting ripe." He held his nose.

"You get kind of used to it. I don't notice it anymore when I go into his house." Cady didn't mention that Pete had a smell similar to cheese, real gamey.

"He says we might go commercial and make some money if I'd do my share."

As Pete talked on and on, Cady quit listening. Once he thought he heard a bark. He started thinking of the fox and the man. He wanted to go looking for them, but he didn't want Pete to go with him. This game he played with the man was something of his own, hidden somewhere in a secret part of himself that he couldn't share. He pretended to be reading again, and didn't answer Pete's questions. Finally Pete noticed and quit talking, and soon he left.

Cady followed the path to the man's house. The path was overgrown with thistle and wild raspberries that caught at his pants. He was in a sweat by the time he got near the clearing.

He waited to get his breath, then slowly crept closer to the house. He pushed into the heaviest part of the brush. After waiting a few minutes, he stooped down and separated the branches, looking through the opening directly at the door. His legs began to feel numb from the crouched position. Cady had just about given up and was ready to go home when suddenly the door opened. The man looked out but he didn't come any farther, as if, with an animal's awareness, he sensed he was not alone. He shut the door quickly. Cady was afraid he had been seen, but it was the man's face that made him turn and run. The lines in the man's face were like crevices in the earth, deep and unfathomable, and his eyes were dark and hooded. It was the grief he saw in the man's face that frightened Cady most.

That night Cady sat in the dark in his room and stared out the window. He was glad for the presence of the old man and woman in the pictures on the wall. He tried to see beyond the pond out to the edge of the jack pines. He wanted to see the fox dance again, and to hear the man laugh.

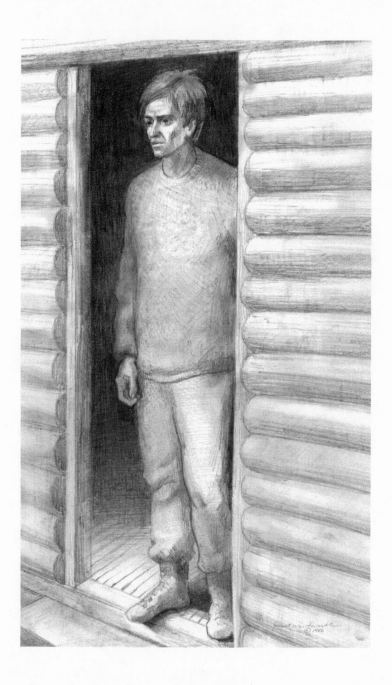

III

Instead of Cady helping Pete with his schoolwork, it was Thea who did. Starting in the middle of November, Pete came over once a week. On the seventeenth of November Cady received a birthday card from Marrietta with a letter tucked in it. Although he had written her several letters, this was the first time she had answered. He remembered she was never good at writing letters, but she had sent cards with mushy verses. He felt tears in back of his eyes when he read her note:

Dear Cady and Thea,
I received your letter. Thanx! The money, to. Thanx! I am working now full time days at the Busy Bee. Jenny goes to a day care center. She likes it. After you left Jenny looked for you Cady. She couldn't understand you had gone away. I try to explain to her. I tell her maybe we'll get to see you again. Nobody has

asked questions about you. That's good isn't it Thea. I would have written you if anyone had come looking. I am sending a package with sox in it. I bought them at Penney's. If they don't fit send them back.

All my love,
Marrietta
X X X X X X

Thea explained about the money. "I send her some once in a while." She shrugged. "I would like to do more."

That night, after Pete finished working his fractions, Thea invited him to stay for supper. She surprised Cady with a huge chocolate cake with candles. Pete and Thea sang "Happy Birthday," and Thea gave Cady a sweatshirt with the words "Minnesota Gophers" across the front. When he tried to thank her, she shrugged as she had about the money she gave to Marrietta. It seemed to Cady he had been here a long time with Thea, and that thirteen was old.

It snowed the week of Thanksgiving. In the night it came, floating low to the earth, bringing a white silence to the woods and fields. On the way to the bus, Cady walked carefully through the snow so as not to disturb the layers of white. The lane was hidden underneath. The woods were disguised. One side of the trees was white where the snow had blown, and the limbs were bent down. The few remaining leaves were crusted with silver, and shone like stars. Cady wanted more than anything to spend the day there, but he hurried and caught his bus.

Thea came to school for the Thanksgiving program that day. The lower grades gave a play, and the high school choir sang patriotic songs. Cady had been picked to read the Thanksgiving proclamation by the governor. Thea was the first one he noticed when he got up to read. She was sitting near the front. He saw her nod her head, and the slight smile on her face. When he finished he looked at her again. For a second he felt his heart going wild, because of the pride he saw in her face.

There was a party for the kids later in the afternoon. As usual Pete was off by himself, and Cady had to drag him into the gym to get his lemonade, sandwich and cake. Bart, the big kid, came over to sit with them. Cady found out that he was older than the rest of them, eighteen and a sophomore, because he had been in a car accident and had to miss a lot of school. Bart dropped a big arm across Pete's shoulders, and called him "little buddy." Pete seemed quite high-spirited and excited, showing off, Cady thought. But it was only to hide how miserable he was feeling, because he turned to Cady suddenly and said he had a letter from Velda to wish him a happy Thanksgiving. He gulped over the words, and his eyes got blurry. "In the letter Ma said to tell me hello, anyway Velda said she did. But they sure as heck ain't expecting me to come home."

Cady tried to cheer Pete up on the bus, and when one of the kids called Pete a goof, Cady slugged him on the arm with his fist as he was getting off. It was almost dark when he started up the lane, but he could see his tracks there, unbroken in the snow, as neat as he had left them, marching between the wheel marks of Thea's car. They followed through the trees like a pattern of fine stitching. Halfway to the house he saw other tracks crossing his, small marks like a dotted line. It was an animal with small feet, maybe the fox, Cady thought, and he plunged off in the direction of the tracks. He went well beyond the pond and his cave, following the tracks up the ridge that lay in back of the pond. He hadn't quite reached the top when he heard a wild yelp, a sound of pain.

The hair rose up on Cady's arms. He went quietly, moving more carefully, stopping every few steps to listen. There was no sound now. He started walking faster. When he heard the yelp again, it was so close that Cady jumped. It seemed directly beneath him. Forgetting all caution Cady dove for what looked like a pile of brush. He pulled at it, jerking the branches apart. He leaned over, almost disappearing into a hole. It was unearthly quiet again. He saw a dark form the size of a small dog. It was hanging upside down by one foot. When he looked closer, he saw the bushy tail of the little fox. It didn't move. He gingerly touched the animal. He saw the chain holding the trap. Cady looked for something to open the trap with. He ran back to the ridge for a rock. He found a large one, spear shaped. When he got back to the hole, he went down on his knees and leaned far down into it.

He saw the jaws of the trap that was holding the fox by the leg. Cady knew about traps. He had seen animals in them before. He pressed the stone down against the spring, releasing the jaws. Making sure it would hold, he slowly backed away from the hole. He waited, holding his breath. Suddenly a small dark figure leaped from the hole. For an instant Cady saw it in the moonlight—like a small shadow cast by a fast-moving cloud. Running on three legs, it disappeared into the trees. There were tears in Cady's eyes, and he felt as if he were floating above the ground.

Another form stepped out from the shadows, large this time. Cady heard a whistle and an answering bark. He wasn't sure, but he thought the man waved to him before he turned. In case the man could hear him, Cady yelled, "I'd like to catch the guy who did this, and hang him by his toes in a trap just like this one!" There was no answer. Cady went back to the hole, dug the trap out of the soft ground, and hid it farther on down the bluff.

Pete was waiting for him when he got home, a big grin on his face. He couldn't keep his eyes off the counter where Thea had two pumpkin pies cooling. "You're coming to our house for Thanksgiving. Did you know that? We're having venison just like the old Pilgrims did." He gave Cady a good-natured cuff. "Where've you been?"

"They had turkey," Cady said, referring to the Pilgrims. "I'd rather." His mind was still on the fox, and it made him short-tempered.

After Pete had gone, Thea put supper on the table. Cady decided not to tell her about the fox, not now anyhow. Instead he talked about the school program, and the little kid who fell off the stage and went home and no one noticed he was gone until his mother screamed he wasn't in the program. And he told her about Bart, who had been hurt in a car accident, and who wanted to be his friend.

Thea worked on the Thanksgiving menu between bites of food, listing what she was bringing to go with the venison that Ingvald was furnishing. She wrinkled her nose.

"It won't smell like Thanksgiving," she said.

"It will smell like cheese."

"Rotten cheese." They both laughed. "And strong meat." Thea threw out her hands. "I cannot eat venison! I won't eat venison. It is probably one of my deer, too. Ingvald doesn't shoot them, but his tenant does. I'd better not catch him!"

Cady wondered if it was his tenant who trapped, too. But he didn't ask.

12

Thea was typing later that evening when she suddenly jumped up, covered the typewriter and put away the manuscript she was working on. "We will kill and dress a chicken. I will not eat deer!"

In the barn she lighted a lantern, and held it high so they could see the chickens roosting in the corner over the stalls. There were eleven chickens. Most of them didn't remove their heads from under their wings, but one started up a hysterical clucking. Thea grabbed that one and handed it to Cady. The chicken hung upside down, twisting and squawking. Cady couldn't take his eyes off it. It was the only white one, the silly chicken he had watched the first day, that never got to the food first. The daffy chicken that laid her eggs in the craziest places.

Thea found the axe and they went out to the yard. She pointed to the large block of wood on a tree stump, and handed Cady the axe. The chicken thrashed around and fell off the block when Cady lost his hold.

He dived after it and grasped it again, his hands around its thighs. He felt the warmth of its body, and the softness of the underfeathers, and the way the old crazy chicken was throbbing with life. Cady laid it back across the block. He leaned over it, holding it by the legs again. He couldn't kill the chicken. When he looked up Thea was watching him, her hands on her hips.

"It's hard, isn't it?" she said. When he threw down the axe, she picked it up. She was mad. She grabbed the chicken from him, and flopped it down on the block. She held it with one hand and raised the other hand with the axe in it. She stood there for a moment, her face turned away. Before she could come down with the axe Cady grabbed her arm. "You don't want to, either. That chicken is a pain in the neck. I've been watching it. I don't think anything ever came out right for it. It's a born loser."

A strange expression crossed Thea's face. "Now here, here, a born loser, you say. What a funny thing to say about a chicken. There's no such thing."

"Couldn't we have something in place of chicken?"

She held the chicken out at arm's length. "No one is a born loser, and certainly not this chicken." She spit out the words. "I never did like to do it. I just grit my teeth and do it. I never killed a chicken until I came out here alone. I've had to do lots of things I didn't like." Her breath came in white puffs of frost. The lantern lighted her face and made her eyes black. "And I don't want you to be a lily-livered sissy!"

"I'm not a lily-livered sissy, but I'm not going to kill that chicken. And I don't want you to. If you do I won't eat it. And I don't like being called names. The Hawk called me enough!"

After a long hard look at Cady, Thea picked up the lantern and walked back to the barn with the chicken dangling at her side. "What a thing to quarrel about," she said.

"I don't want things said against me, like they were about my father," Cady called after her, and he turned and ran into the house.

When she followed him in, she sat down in a kitchen chair. She unbuttoned her coat and let it drape across the back. "You're right, you know," she said. "I didn't think of how it sounded. I wouldn't say anything against you, or your father."

Cady decided it was time to tell Thea about the fox. "Who traps on your land?" he asked.

"No one that I know."

"That tenant farmer who kills deer—would he?"

"Could be. I wouldn't be surprised. Why do you ask?"

"Tonight I let a fox out of the trap. It was hurt."

Thea quickly rose from her chair, picked up her coat and was in the pantry hanging it up before she asked, "How badly was it hurt?"

"One leg was hurt, but it could run on the other three."

"That's good," she said, relief in her voice. "I mean that it could run away."

"Why would I be mean enough to kill a chicken, if I let a fox out of a trap? I just don't like anything to die. It's my way of thinking. So don't ever call me a sissy again. I won't stay here."

"I understand—I understand." She rubbed her cheek nervously. She walked to the refrigerator and looked

86

in. "We'll have ham in place of chicken," she said. Cady saw how troubled she was.

The next morning, when Thea was packing the food to take to Ingvald's, Cady noticed she left out some of the ham and sweet potatoes, and one of the fresh pies was left on the counter. When she saw Cady watching her, she became flustered. "There's always another day coming," she said.

She drove the old Plymouth out the back way to the road. As they came to Cady's tracks, where he had turned off to follow the fox, she slowed down and looked in the direction he had gone.

Pete and Ingvald rushed out to the car with the goats to help Cady and Thea carry the food into the house. Ingvald wouldn't let Pete carry the big picnic basket, but he laughed good-naturedly when he took it from him. "Big feet trip. Just keep the goats from going in the house with us," he said.

The house had a warm smell. Cady's sensitive nose picked out the cheesy odor absorbed into the pipe smoke, and the gamey smell of venison smothered in onions. The couch had been pushed out of the front room, and the table put in the center. The white tablecloth was off-color, and slightly wrinkled, like Pete's shirts. The dishes were all sizes and colors, but in the center of the table was a beautiful hand-carved pheasant.

Ingvald wouldn't let Thea help with anything, but he kept Pete and Cady busy. He put his venison and dressing by his place at the head of the table. When they were seated, he served everyone a helping without asking them if they wanted any. The rest of the food was passed around and around until they had finished the pumpkin pie.

The talk at the table was slow and lazy. Cady thought of Thanksgiving last year with Marrietta and Jenny, of smelling chicken and dressing drifting up the stairs from the landlady's, while they ate a hamburger apiece, and a stale pie that the Busy Bee had given to Marrietta. They had eaten with the lights out, and a candle in the middle of the table, and Jenny tried to touch the flame and laughed. Later they danced to the radio with Jenny tucked between them. Now it made Cady smile and feel close to them.

After Pete and Cady helped Ingvald clean up the dishes, they went sliding on the slope in back of the barn.

Thea and Cady drove home in the late afternoon. From the east the moon hung like a child's balloon afire. Because the sky was still light, Thea suggested they walk out and pick out their Christmas tree when they got home. After she had put the food away she found an old towel from which she tore a long strip to mark the tree.

Thea led the way out past the pond to where young pines grew. They took almost an hour to decide. Cady wanted the tall one that would touch the ceiling, and Thea wanted the short, squatty one. They compromised on a medium-tall, thick one that would fill the corner near the fireplace. "You can come back a few days before Christmas and cut it, Cady," Thea said, as she tied the orange towel to a branch. "On Christmas Eve we will decorate it." She walked around the tree again. "Only I never like to cut down trees. It seems so disrespectful. A tree has such dignity, don't you think so?" She looked at Cady. "And it is a living thing," she said. "Isn't that true?" She turned suddenly to Cady. "Does it suit you? You do like the tree?"

"Yes."

"Is it your first tree?"

He nodded his head, then spoke. "Yes."

"I'm glad we found it together." Her voice had the light bell sound that Cady liked. "And we did agree on it, didn't we?" she said.

In the half-light he could not see much of her face, except that she smiled. Cady felt a twinge that could have been one of pain or excitement, or maybe both. When he and Thea talked it was more than words. It was an understanding, one word balanced on another to give it special meaning.

Thea took Cady's arm as they walked home. It had turned bitter cold. The world had crystallized, turning the stars into ice chips, and the snow under their feet crackled like broken glass.

13

For two days Cady fought the urge to go out to see the man. He thought he'd better have a good reason, if he wasn't to be tossed out of the man's cabin. For himself, he had several reasons to go. One was to see if the fox in the trap belonged to the man, and if its leg was healing. Another reason was to try to learn why the food Thea had left on the counter Thanksgiving Day had disappeared while they were gone.

On Sunday afternoon Cady told Thea he was going out to see if he could still find his cave since the snow. The sharpness of the air quickened his walk to a run. The wind was blowing hard, shaking the trees and chasing shadows across the ground. Far off Cady heard the strident call of a blue jay. Some distance behind his cave he found footprints in the snow, coming from the direction of the cabin and returning to it. He followed them along the edge of the field, toward the jack pines.

As he came close to the cabin, he saw smoke coming out of the chimney. He crept into the brush, as he had before, and waited for his breathing to quiet down. He had to force himself to go on. He was determined not to go home until he knew how the fox was. He was sure it belonged to the man. He stepped out into the clearing and walked up to the door. It opened before he had a chance to knock. The man was dressed to go out, in a heavy jacket and hood. As cold as he was, Cady felt sweat on his face. His hands were like lumps of ice, and his tongue caught on the roof of his mouth and wouldn't move.

"Yes?" the man said. "You looking for someone?"

Cady shifted his weight. Then he saw the fox. It was sitting by the fireplace, its tail curled around its body. For a second it laid back its ears. Then, at a sign from the man, it became more friendly. It cocked its head, its face an impudent mask, black nose, white cheeks and throat, eyes like peeled grapes. Cady pointed to the fox. "Has he been hurt?" Cady's eyes slid back to the man, and he was frightened by the intensity of his expression. His eyes were a fierce, fiery blue.

"I didn't ask you to come here." The man closed the door behind Cady. The fox moved up to the man's side and Cady saw the hind leg in a splint.

"It is the one! I took him out of a trap."

"His leg is broken. Was it your trap?"

"No!" The unfairness of it made Cady mad. "You know better. You were there that night when I released the fox. Why are you pretending you weren't?"

"Why have you been bothering around here, boy?"

"Because I've got a right to."

"Where do you live?"

"I live with Thea."

The man took off his hood and jacket, and threw them over a chair. "I don't know any Thea." The man kept his face turned, and Cady couldn't see his eyes, but he knew he was lying.

"I only came to see if the fox was all right. I'd think you might be glad I did."

"I'm glad for that."

"And I'd think you'd be glad I didn't let the fox tear its leg off."

"Yes." Cady thought that he detected a hint of respect in the man's voice.

"I thought you waved to me that night, else I wouldn't have come."

The man's face was stone. It was impossible for Cady to know what he was thinking. "I might have. Do you want to pet him?" The man looked up at him now. "He's waiting, if you're not afraid."

"I'm not afraid," Cady said. He put out his hand carefully to the fox. He let it sniff at his hand, then he stroked its ears. The fox raised its head and stared back at Cady with golden, inquisitive eyes. "He's like a dog. Where did you get him?"

"I found him when he was just a kit. His mother was killed by a hunter."

"I didn't know you could tame a fox."

"He is tame, isn't he?"

"One day I saw him, quite a long time ago. He was playing—it looked like dancing."

"Animals know more about joy and being free than most people do. How did you know it was this fox? You were bothering around here, weren't you?"

It took all of Cady's courage to answer. "I've followed you and the fox. It took me a while to find you."

"Why?" The muscles along the man's cheekbone moved as if pulled on a string.

"Who are you? Why do you live here on Thea's land?"

The lines deepened in the man's face, touching bone. His eyes didn't lose their fierceness. "Thoreau," he said, looking at Cady from the corner of his eye. "He lived in the woods with unfenced nature to his door, squirrels on his roof and under the floor, and the bark of a fox to awaken him in the night. Not a place for a sane man—would you say? Do you happen to know who Thoreau is?"

Cady nodded. He had learned about him at school. He pointed back toward Thea's house, and the pond. "That isn't Walden Pond."

"So you are saying I cannot be Thoreau?"

Cady slowly shook his head. "I didn't say that, but he must be dead."

"Maybe he is dead. I've forgotten."

Cady looked past the man to the room they were standing in. He saw that one wall was covered with shelves of books. There was one big chair in front of the fireplace. By the table were two handmade benches. On one wall were bunks, one above the other. The windows were uncurtained and full of plants. Past the table he saw a small room that must be the kitchen.

The man followed Cady's eyes without saying anything. Once or twice Cady shifted his weight from one leg to the other. The man didn't offer him a place to sit. The silence was killing him.

93

"You're afraid. You think I'm crazy." The man's voice was dry, rasping. "Because I don't know who I am."

"I'm not afraid. And I think you know who you are. I think I'd better go."

The man opened the door and waited for Cady to leave, the fox sitting between his feet. When he was almost to the edge of the clearing Cady looked back. He heard what the man said, though he wasn't sure if he was meant to. "A man thinking or working is always alone, let him be where he will." It sounded as if he were reading the words.

14

The next few days Cady looked at Thea with different eyes. He was sure now he knew where the pie and ham had gone on Thanksgiving day. He waited for her to give something away. She'd have to be the first one to admit she knew about the man, not Cady. She seemed distracted and absentminded, going about the house doing some things over twice and leaving other things undone. She had always been watchful of him, but now it seemed to Cady that she studied him as she might a strange species from another planet.

On the day school was to let out early for clerical day, she suggested he get off the bus in town and do some Christmas shopping. She gave him ten dollars and told him to start walking home, and she would pick him up at five.

Cady went to his room after his wallet. He folded his ten-dollar bill and put it next to the one that Marrietta had given him, on top, so he would remember which was which. He felt rich. He asked Pete to stop in town with him. At noon, when they got off the bus, they went to Kinsith's Department Store. Cady thought it looked more like a flea market. Everything was mixed together and messy. Pete raised his head and sniffed like a bird dog at the smell of licorice, leather goods and fresh-ground coffee. He touched the leather belts, and rubbed his hand over the ties, pulling a green and blue one out to get a closer look. He began to wander up and down the aisles. Cady walked close behind him.

"Remember, no shoplifting. I'm responsible," he whispered to Pete. Pete looked at Cady with terrible disappointment in his eyes. Mr. Hicock, over in the grocery section, recognized Cady from the time he had come in with Thea. He gave the boys a long steady stare, and followed along behind them. Cady stopped at the jewelry counter and examined the pearls in purple velvet boxes, and the short strings of red and blue beads for little girls.

"You look to be buying some beads?" Mr. Hicock asked. He was a small man with a skinny neck and a quivering chin. Cady knew his kid in school who weighed over two hundred pounds.

"We'll have Cokes while we're looking," Cady said.

Mr. Hicock told them they'd have to drink them in the grocery section. While the boys sipped their drinks, he leaned on the glass case. He had a flimsy mustache, and he looked like a wasp. "Do you like it here with Mrs. McVey? I understand you're a relative."

"Guess so." Cady had a hard time keeping a grin off his face. He liked playing that game of Thea's, telling the truth and not telling the truth.

"Going to stay long?" The man stared at Cady hard enough to make him uncomfortable. "It seems a boy like you would want to be with his family—got one?" It was suddenly no longer a game for Cady. He didn't have to answer anyone's questions. He took a drink of Coke.

"Where're you from?"

"The south." Cady banged down his money on the glass case.

"I'm from Minneapolis, and Ingvald is my uncle," Pete said.

"Let's go." Cady was already halfway out the door.

They walked toward a gang of kids horsing around in front of the tavern. Cady tried to skirt around them, prodding Pete ahead of him. Pete was so busy trying to swig on the bottle of Coke, he couldn't see where he was going. Cady was still upset by the prying of Mr. Hicock. It could almost turn a person into a liar.

Cady didn't see it happen until Pete went down over the curb, landing on his back in the street. A letter he had written to Velda flew out of his pocket into the brown slush, soaking it, smearing the address. One of the kids stepped on it before he could pick it up. Still on the ground, Pete grabbed the kid's ankle, and Cady pushed him over.

Cady saw tears come to Pete's eyes as he tried to wipe off his letter, and a sob like the baying of a hound came out before Pete could control it. Then the kids started in on him. One called him Horse Ears. Cady couldn't stand to see Pete so helpless, his eyes watery and frightened. And when the kids laughed, Cady went blind mad, whirling in a circle, punching everyone in his way. He saw old Spiketooth egging them all on—his shrill screaming sounded like the Hawk to Cady. He hit again, hard enough to make someone moan.

Cady heard another voice. "You're killing them." It was Bart. He reached in with his long arms and scattered the kids like mice. They started disappearing like getting sucked into a manhole. "You're pretty tough." Bart laughed gently.

He walked with them to mail Pete's letter. In the post office Cady straightened his clothes, tucking in his shirt and trying to hide the rip in the sleeve of his jacket. Bart left them back at Kinsith's. Cady went straight to the jewelry counter and looked at the pearls again. He found a string for nine dollars and ninety-five cents. Next he went to the books and toys. Reading snatches from picture books, he decided on one with pop-up characters for Jenny. When he started for the underwear counter, Pete was following close behind him, and Mr. Hicock behind Pete, so he left that for Thea to buy for Marrietta. Mr. Hicock gift wrapped the pearls and the book without a word, except to tell Cady the price.

When they started walking home, the road was freezing and getting slick. A wind had come up and they pulled their collars up around their necks.

"I didn't like what you said in the store to me about shoplifting. I'm not making any more trouble—just remember that. I didn't think you'd say that to me." Pete had a tremor in his voice that Cady had never heard before.

"I didn't mean anything by it."

"You told me not to shoplift."

"Nobody heard it."

"I did."

"I was looking out for you." Cady was half mad at Pete.

"You don't need to, and I ain't looking for marijuana out at Ingvald's field, either. In case you think so." Pete's eyes were troubled. "I can't stand everyone thinking I can't do things—that I'm dumb. That's what the kids thought today, because I'm slow in school. They think they can treat me any old way. Well, they can't."

"I don't think that." Cady put his hand on Pete's shoulder.

"Act like it, then." He pulled away from Cady.

"Okay, I will."

"I'm trying to act like Ingvald expects me to. I got a plan. I figure if I work hard enough helping him, maybe I can fix it so Velda can come. That's what I told her in the letter."

"That'd be nice." Cady's shame blurred his words. He had forgotten that you could hurt someone in such a small way. He had forgotten about Thea calling him sissy. He had never had to deal with close relationships until he had come to live with Thea.

"That was okay, what you did for me when I got pushed down. But you didn't have to get in a fight because of me. I'm sorry you got hurt, and that you tore your jacket. I'm sorry. I'm sorry!" Pete was running away from him now, sliding on the ice along the side of the road.

They saw Thea coming in the old Plymouth through the dusk, the flickering headlights making long spears of light. After they dropped Pete off, Thea turned to Cady and looked at his scratched cheek and his torn sleeve. "What on earth happened to you?"

"A fight."

"How did it happen?"

"We didn't start it. Someone pushed Pete down. They called him names." Cady shrugged. "That was it."

"That was it, huh?" Thea mimicked his voice. "Who won?"

A slow grin spread across Cady's face. "I think we did—with Bart's help. I got in some pretty good pokes."

"Tell me about it."

"The kids called him Horse Ears."

"What a miserable name to call him."

"I thought so, but he couldn't handle it."

"And you can handle yourself?"

Cady looked to see if Thea was being sarcastic. She wasn't: Her eyes were serious, intent, as if his answer was important.

"I think I did. I was mad. I wasn't afraid. It was the only thing I knew to do." He glanced at Thea. "I guess I wasn't even thinking."

"You didn't feel like running away?"

"If I did, I forgot it."

"I might have done the same thing myself." She looked smaller to Cady behind the steering wheel, her face not swerving from the road, only her eyes looking out the corner at Cady, once in a while. The dash lights showed that she was smiling. "It's funny what makes us do things. I was a tomboy, and I got mad easily. One time I took the town bully down and half killed him." Thea laughed at herself. Sleet was hitting the windshield now, making it hard to see. She was sitting with her chin almost resting on the steering wheel. "I hated that kid."

"I hate the Hawk, my aunt Josephine. She's mean. That's why I fought today. I could see her right there in front of me."

Thea had quit smiling.

"She was unfair. She did things to hurt me. I think I always wanted to hit her."

"What did she do to you?"

"She said things about my father. She said I was spineless like him. She wanted me to hate him."

"But you don't, do you?"

"How can you hate someone you don't know?"

"Impossible." Thea seemed pleased. She patted Cady on the knee, then concentrated on keeping them steady on the slippery road.

15

It had been a week since Cady had seen the man and the fox. When he awoke on Sunday morning, early, the first thing he thought of was the fox. He saw it hanging again from the trap. If it hadn't been for him finding it when he did, it probably would have died. He wondered how many other animals had been trapped in the woods. He crawled to the foot of his bed and looked out the window, trying to see past the pond to the cliffs where he had found the trap. And he looked beyond that to the place where the trees were huge, sheltering the clearing where the man lived. After they had eaten dinner, Cady told Thea he was going out to look for traps.

"If you find one, get rid of it, but be careful," she said. She poured herself another cup of coffee, and sat again at the table. "Dress warmly." She was pensive and quiet, her eyes searching his face, full of questions but not asking.

He went up the ridge, back to the place he had

found the fox. He located the hole where the trap had been set. It was empty. But he had gone only another twenty feet when he saw a suspicious mound of brush. He pushed some of the branches aside and saw it was covering a hole, and inside the hole was an empty trap. He picked up a broken tree limb and threw it into the hole, springing the trap. Then he worked quickly, pulling at the stake and the chain that held it. He hauled it all up out of the hole, the trap holding the piece of tree limb in its grip. Dragging it after him, he started in the direction of the man's cabin.

This time Cady might have been expected. Or he might have been seen from a window. The door opened before he had crossed the clearing. The man looked from him to the trap.

"Where did you get that?" he asked.

"I wanted to see if that guy was trapping again. I thought he might have it the same place. It was near."

"Nothing in it?"

Cady grinned. "Only this big stick, which I put in it. I thought maybe you'd like it. The trap, I mean."

"I'll take care of it. I'll put it where he'll never find it again. If you're cold, you can come in," the man said brusquely. He motioned Cady into the cabin.

"Haul off your coat and get a seat there on the bench, if you've got a minute." He brought Cady a big, thick mug of coffee. "You can freeze to death out there. Do you know that?"

"I don't want to bother you."

"You're not. I'll tell you when you are. I expect you think you did something for me." Cady thought he saw mockery in his eyes.

"No, for the fox." Cady looked around for him then. The fox was curled up in the shadow under the bunk bed, not moving, its tail curled around its face. It paid no attention to Cady. Its leg was still in a splint. "Is he all right?"

"He's coming. I'm surprised he got caught in a trap. I doubt he will again. A fox's sense of touch is so sensitive he can catch insects by feeling them in the high grass. When the fox learns the danger of traps, he uses his sense of touch to locate the traps, and he digs them out."

"Who's setting the traps?"

"I don't know. I never see anyone around. I've been looking for them. If I did . . ."

The man stopped talking. He poked the fire and threw on more wood. He got himself a cup of coffee, and sat down opposite Cady. The man looked at Cady so long and so hard that Cady had a bad time just holding his mouth straight. He didn't know whether to get up and leave, or see if the man would talk to him some more. He wanted to stay.

"Were there others?" Cady nodded in the fox's direction.

"There were two dead ones outside their den. Killed by a gun butt."

Cady couldn't help shuddering. The man noticed— Cady could tell by a lightening of his eyes for just a moment. "Is that the way they killed the mother?" Cady asked.

The man nodded his head. "The vixen was dead. Usually there's a male that helps look after the kits, but he was gone. Their den was on the edge of the field on a knoll. I think it belonged to a woodchuck once before they took it over. They do that."

"Do you think the male is dead?"

"It's hard to tell. He just disappeared." The man's voice was monotonous. His mouth twisted as he talked. "After they mate they are very affectionate to each other, and devoted to their offspring. I've heard tell that the mate will lie near a trapped fox, unwilling to save itself and leave the vixen to her fate." The man's face looked weary, and he stopped talking.

It became an easy silence for Cady. The man acted as though he was hardly aware that Cady was there. Cady sipped his coffee. The fire had warmed him to a sleepy state. Through half-closed lids Cady studied the man. He was long and terribly thin. His wild red hair stood on end. His fierce blue eyes still startled Cady.

Cady got up and went over to the fox. At first it flattened its ears in a threatening way, but as Cady made a soft clucking sound, its ears came up and it cocked its head and waited. Cady spoke without thinking, disturbing the man, he could see. "What's its name?"

"Reynard. What else? Named by the poets." He went to the big chair by the fire and swiveled it around where he could watch the flames, his back to Cady. "You speak of man, and it includes all men. You speak of Reynard, and it is all foxes. Does that make sense to you?"

"No." Cady sat cross-legged in front of the fox. He stroked its head, carefully but with authority. The fox lay quiet. The man had turned again to face Cady.

Silence stretched between the three of them. Cady was aware of how closely the man watched him, but somehow he didn't mind.

Almost an hour passed before Cady knew he must leave. While he put on his coat and cap, the man sat quietly in his chair. He did not speak again. "Good-by, Mr. Thoreau," Cady said. The man's eyebrows went up. "I like your fox." Cady waited for an answer, but there was none.

Cady followed his own tracks home. It was a windless night. The moon had just come up over the trees. The huge jack pines seemed to hang solemnly from the sky. Cady noticed that the shadows of the trees took on the shapes of men—a formation of men marching together in step. A solitary owl screeched from the top of one of the trees. The sound was almost human—forlorn and lonely, reminding Cady of the man.

Thea looked up from her reading when he came into the kitchen. For an instant she took him in, first his face, his eyes, then down to his feet, as if she might determine where he had been. But she didn't ask, for which Cady was thankful. She fixed bacon and eggs for them, and toast and strawberry jam.

That night Cady dreamed of the fox. He was trying to catch it, but it ran. He followed the fox through the woods, up the ridge to the trap. He saw the dead mother and the kits, and the mate lay close beside them and howled.

16

The second week of December Thea and Cady went into town. They spent most of the afternoon in Kinsith's Department Store. Thea did Christmas shopping, and she sent Cady to the tavern for a hamburger once to get him out of the way while she bought his present. They spent another hour in the grocery section, buying ten pounds of sugar, and packages of coconut, chocolate chips and nuts. On the way home they stopped at Ingvald's to get several pounds of butter and a quart of cream. "From your Jersey cows, not your goats," Thea warned Ingvald.

That night she hurried supper and asked Cady to do the dishes. She put bowls, spoons and a measuring cup on the counter, the things she had bought in the afternoon, two heavy pans and a wooden spoon. She measured and mixed while Cady watched in fascination. First she made peanut brittle and two pans of penuche. Cady helped her store it in the cold little pantry off the kitchen. Next she made divinity and fudge. Thea worked with a concentration and determination that was hard for Cady to understand. Sometimes she smiled to herself, and other times she had a sad faraway look, moving out away from him. Cady blistered his hands from beating the fudge. She poured the chocolate into buttered pans in swirls and waves, and she made the divinity into peaks.

It was midnight before they were through. Thea made them peanut butter sandwiches and tea, and she cut a piece of fudge for each of them. She leaned on her elbows, her face framed in her hands, taking bites and chewing slowly on her sandwich. "I've not made candy for years," she said.

"Why did we make so much? I'll bet we've got at least ten pounds. What will we do with it?"

"Maybe we've got ten pounds. I'll give some away." She looked at him sharply. "Have you had that much candy lately? Would you like to get sick on it just once?" She surprised him when she talked that way, with an intensity that made what she said sound more important than it was. Doubletalk was what Cady called it.

"I'd like to get real sick on candy, enough to make me throw up," he said.

"That's more like it," she said. "Now you sound normal. I'd like to send some to Marrietta and Jenny, in their Christmas box."

Cady was tired. He laid his head on the table and listened to Thea talk about Christmas and the cookies and *julekake* she had yet to bake. He swallowed a yawn so Thea wouldn't push him off to bed. He'd rather sit here all night with Thea, full of the spirit that made him warm and happy.

As Christmas came nearer she decorated the house by bits and dribbles. In the attic she had found five red paper bells. Cady noticed they were a little torn, but when she opened them and fluffed them and pushed the torn edges out of sight, they didn't look bad. She hung them on strings from the light fixtures. She looked over her shoulder at Cady. "Now if you think it's crazy putting these old things up . . . do you know how old these bells are? My brother and I always put them up. It's just part of Christmas, putting up the bells." She shrugged to hide her feelings.

That night they packed a box for Marrietta and Jenny. Thea had bought the underwear for Marrietta, and a small doll for Jenny. Into the pocket of a blouse for Marrietta she was wrapping, she slipped a twenty-dollar bill. Then they packed as much candy as there was room left in the box.

One day, the week before school let out for Christmas vacation, Pete was bursting when Cady got on the bus. He waved a letter at him. "It's from Velda," he said. Before Cady could plop down beside him on the seat, Pete held the letter in front of his nose. "She's coming. Ingvald said she could. At first I was going home, but Ingvald said he'd get lonely, and Velda might as well come here. Anyway, my mom has a new boyfriend, and she's going to his place for Christmas. She'll take DeDe. Velda'd be in the way, she says."

Cady looked closely at Pete to see if he was really as tickled as he said, or if he was hurt. But Pete was grinning. "You'll like Velda," he said. "At first you might think she's kind of funny, but after you get to know her, you'll get a kick out of her." He licked at the bubbles of spit at the corners of his mouth. "She can draw anything. That's what she's always doing. We only fight half of the time." He stretched his mouth wide, laughing.

Thea and Cady took Ingvald and Pete to the bus station to meet Velda. Velda was the last one to get off the bus. She jumped off the steps and landed against Pete, almost knocking him down. She was small, half a head shorter than Pete. Cady couldn't figure her age. Her red coat was dirty, and it came to the tops of her boots. A red cap hung over one ear, exposing the pale blond hair that strung down her back like a horse's mane. Her pale face made her freckles stand out like specks of dirt on a window. She had a square jaw and a pug nose, and she wore one long earring and one button earring.

"Did you get my letter that I was coming?" She nudged Pete's arm. She had a little whispery voice.

"Why else would I be here?" Pete rolled his eyes at Cady.

She suddenly noticed the others. She stepped behind Pete, hanging on to his hand, but she went on talking nervously. "I kept thinking what would I do if you weren't here. And maybe you didn't get my letter."

All at once Ingvald patted her on the shoulder, and Thea took her hand and managed to pull her clear of Pete, explaining she and Cady were Pete's friends. Velda smiled weakly. She put her arm through Pete's again and hung on tight. Her face turned blood red, and she ducked her head at each one in the circle, then clammed up.

When Thea let them out of the car, Pete and Velda

ran on ahead of Ingvald for the house, Pete jerking her along by the hand. Cady felt a tugging at his insides as he watched the way they hung onto each other.

Two days before Christmas Eve, Thea sent Cady out into the woods to cut down the pine tree that he and Thea had picked. He walked past the pond to the grove of young pines. It took him a while to find the orange cloth tied to their tree. The last snow had almost hidden it. He looked for other tracks in the snow. He hadn't seen the man for several days. Twice he had started in that direction, but stopped when he remembered the man had not spoken when Cady left, had not asked him to come back.

Cady removed the orange flag from the branch. The tree stood like a tent covered with snow, and the earth, protected underneath, was bare. Cady crawled under, lying flat. At first it seemed quiet to him and he heard nothing. Then the silence was filled with so many voices, it was hard to sift one from the other—the small sounds of the wind, the shifting of the branches, the snapping of the ice on the needles. Cady considered the pain of destroying something alive. Thea had expressed something like that when they had picked the tree out, he remembered. "But then, it's too close to the others," she had said later. "It wouldn't grow big anyway." When he gave the last whack and the tree fell, Cady was sure he saw a final shudder.

His mood had changed by the time he carried it back to the house and made a stand for it. The tree was a beauty from every side. "We won't have to worry about hiding the bad side," Thea said, as she brought a pail of water to set the tree in. On Christmas Eve they decorated it.

Thea was up early the next morning, before Cady. It was already beginning to smell like turkey by the time he got up. He noticed there were no gifts under the tree. No need to worry yet—his gift for Thea was still up in his drawer.

She put a pot of coffee and a huge loaf of *julekake* in the middle of the table. The bread was frosted and had cherries on top, and looked more like dessert. She cut them thick slices and poured them coffee. She pushed the butter across to him. "This is all you're getting until we eat this afternoon," she said. She sipped her coffee quietly, her eyes filled with thoughts. Once she got ready to say something to him, but she didn't. Instead she looked across the table at him with concern. Cady felt like a flea on the end of a pin. He hunched over his plate. Whatever was coming, he didn't want to hear it while he was eating.

Later he helped her pull the table out from the wall and put in two leaves, making it long enough for several people. He knew she had invited Ingvald and Pete and Velda. "I don't want those poor kids to have to eat venison for Christmas," she explained.

"Or goat's cheese," Cady added.

She set the table with a linen cloth and linen napkins and crystal goblets that Cady had never seen. The plates and cups and saucers all matched, and shone like they had been polished. Thea hummed all the time she was working.

Suddenly she said, "I suppose you noticed we've made the table larger, and I am setting it for six." She walked about the table, laying out the silverware. She didn't look at Cady. "We're having one other person besides Ingvald and the children for dinner. I don't like anyone to be left out on Christmas Day. Do you?" She looked at Cady then. "This man lives alone out on the edge of our property." It was the first time that Cady had ever seen her blush like this. "I invited him to eat with us." She paused. "I don't imagine you know who I'm talking about." She sat down in a chair as if the air had gone out of her. "Do you?" Her eyes reached into his mind, trying to pick out what he was thinking. He shook his head and left the house to feed the chickens.

He didn't go near Thea until he heard Pete's voice. He and Ingvald were helping Thea make a fire in the fireplace. Thea glanced at him when Cady came into the room, but then paid no attention to him. Cady was in the kitchen helping Velda when the door opened and the man came in without knocking. He took off his hat and coat and hung them in the pantry, as if he knew his way around. When he came back into the kitchen Cady was waiting for him. He pulled out a chair at the table.

"Would you like a cup of coffee, Mr. Thoreau?" Cady hoped the man would pass it off with a laugh, but he didn't. He was stone faced, as if he had never heard the name. Velda stopped peeling potatoes and looked at Cady as if he were crazy. He tried to jog the man's memory again. "The fox's leg, is it better?"

"He's coming along."

"Thea's expecting you. She told me you were coming this morning." Cady couldn't control his tongue—the man made him nervous. He poured him a cup of coffee, and the man carried it into the front room. Cady watched through the door as Thea nodded to him. There was no hint that he had ever seen Cady before, but there was something between the man and Thea. Cady could feel it. He saw it in their eyes. He saw Thea's lips tremble for a moment, then she composed herself and managed to look fairly calm when she spoke to him. She called him Mr. Lowell, and introduced him around until she got to Cady. She called him from behind the door. She smiled uneasily from one to the other, as if that was introduction enough.

The man remained poker-faced all through dinner. He rarely spoke except to answer Ingvald or Thea. Cady would have felt very uncomfortable if it hadn't been for Velda and Pete. They giggled all the time—when one started, the other joined in. Velda had warmed to Thea, and she was much less shy than Pete. The words flowed from her mouth like water running from a spring. She brought them all up to date on the actions of DeDe, her baby brother, and how her mom met her new boyfriend at the Laundromat. She hoped they'd get married. "It would serve them both right," she said.

When they had finished with the turkey and the trimmings, Thea cleared the table and whipped the cream that Ingvald had brought for the pumpkin pie. Later in the afternoon Cady took Velda and Pete out to his cave. They built a fire and ate Thea's peanut brittle.

Ingvald was waiting for them when they got back to the house. It seemed to Cady that he bundled Velda and Pete off in a big hurry. Cady was surprised, too, that Mr. Lowell stayed on. Thea insisted Cady not help her finish up, but keep the man company in the front room. It was getting colder outside. They pulled their chairs close to the fire. The man rested his chin in his hand. He made no effort to talk. His eyes followed Thea whenever she came into the room. When she had finished removing the leaves from the table and pushing it against the wall, she came and sat with them, but for only a moment. She jumped up and went to the kitchen, brought them three small glasses on a tray and poured dark red wine from a decanter. She touched her glass to Cady's.

"To you, Cady. To our first Christmas together." She turned to Mr. Lowell, touching his glass. "What do you wish to toast? What will it be? Will you tell me, or will I have to guess?" She laughed softly, as if at a private joke. Cady noticed the smile did not spread to her eyes. "You know I had to drag him here to be with us, Cady. He has a small piece of my land he lives on. I think Christmas is a time to be together, don't you?"

Cady nodded. He heard the determination in her voice. He looked to see if Mr. Lowell agreed. The man smiled faintly, distantly. It was hard to tell.

"I suppose you've got lots of Christmases you remember," Thea said.

Mr. Lowell shook his head. He swallowed his wine in one gulp. "I don't have memories. Did you forget?"

Thea filled his glass again and sipped at her own wine. When Mr. Lowell had emptied his glass again, she filled it once more. Cady leaned forward and clicked glasses with him. The man's face had taken on some of the flame color of the firelight. He seemed more relaxed. Cady thought he handled himself well for someone who hides in the woods.

"I have memories," Thea said. She leaned her head against the back of her chair, and rested for a moment. She started talking slowly, as if she were telling a dream. "I remember the ferry at Galveston, and the creeping fogs that hid the sunsets, and the big ships that came into port. And the shrimp boats coming in, a cloud of gulls swooping down and taking bread from my hand." She sat quietly for a few minutes with her eyes closed. When she spoke again her voice seemed strained to Cady, nervous. "In Missouri, where I lived before, we didn't have an ocean, but we did have a big pond, like here. When I was little we used to swim there, and in the winter we ice-skated. I had a little brother. He swam like a frog, better than I could. He did everything well." Before Cady could stop her, she told about Cady being swept down the flooded creek,

117

and how he saved himself. "He could swim like a frog, too. He must have. He saved himself."

When Cady looked up he caught the man's eyes for a moment. His eyes were coming alive, as though he did have memories. Cady looked away from him to the tree. There were no lights, but it glowed with Thea's little glass birds set in among the branches, lighted deep within by the firelight. After the first sips of wine Cady found himself watching the little birds. They grew more beautiful to him, and he was filled with a sense of pleasure. He could almost believe they were moving, their wings fluttering.

Mr. Lowell's eyes had closed, and Thea leaned forward, studying him with a small smile on her face. Her arched neck was long and beautiful, and her head was gracefully turned like one of the glass birds on the tree. Cady watched the two of them secretly.

It was a fleeting expression that he caught, around the eyes, the mouth. He looked again and again, from one to the other. They were alike. He looked at Thea's hands folded in her lap, and then down at his own hands holding his glass of wine, at his long slender fingers, as fine boned as Thea's. Gradually came the feeling that somehow all three of them were alike. There was a stirring deep inside Cady. It came in waves. It was hard for him to get his breath.

Cady took his wine glass to the kitchen. He was drawn to the mirror over the sink. His reddish hair was like theirs. His eyes were as blue as Thea's with a fire in them that he had seen in hers and Mr. Lowell's. His brow was wide, and his prominent cheekbones were like theirs, but on him more delicate and rounded. When he returned he glanced at them quickly, but neither had noticed he was gone. When he looked at the tree again, the glass birds moved about in a queer fashion, distorted, and tears came at the corner of his eyes. Then Cady was struck with an extraordinary sense of vision—some secret part of him had known this all along: Somehow they were joined. They were a circle of three, and like the glass birds on the Christmas tree, unable to change—only to reflect—each other.

When the room began to get cool, Cady left them to get more wood. He built up the fire again to roaring flames. While he was gone, Thea had put gifts under the tree, but before they opened them she made popcorn and brought in a plate of fudge. Cady hurried upstairs to get Thea's pearl necklace out of his drawer. It bothered him that he had nothing for Mr. Lowell. He saw the bird that Ingvald had carved for him on the dresser and brought it down with him.

First he gave the wrapped gift to Thea. She smiled broadly at him, and put the pearls around her neck. She put her hand to her throat, touching them. "They're beautiful," she said. And in the firelight Cady thought they looked like real pearls. When he gave the carved bird to Mr. Lowell, he seemed surprised. He looked at it quickly and set it on the arm of his chair. Thea gave gloves, a scarf, and cap with earmuffs to Cady, and a small leather-bound book to Mr. Lowell. When Mr. Lowell opened it, it had blank pages. He seemed surprised again.

"A journal," Thea said, "to keep a record of your days. Some things slip away and we forget." Her voice was gentle.

The last gift under the tree was a small box tied

with a red bow that Thea handed to Cady. Inside was a gold watch, but old, Cady noticed. It was no larger than a silver dollar, and the back of it had tulips and vines and a tiny church etched in the center. Cady pressed it into his palm. It fit there in his hand, smooth.

"My dad's," Thea said. Her eyes were moist, and her face quite pink.

Cady held it out to the man. Mr. Lowell took it and examined it, turning it over in his hand. Then he gave it back to Cady. "I'd have liked that when I was a boy," he said.

After Mr. Lowell left, Cady saw the carved bird he had given him on the chair arm. "He left without the bird I gave him," Cady said to Thea.

"Don't worry about it," she said. She sounded exhausted.

18

For several days after Christmas Thea and Cady avoided talking much to each other. When they did talk, it was only in bits and pieces. Thea never mentioned Mr. Lowell. When Cady tried to talk about him, she immediately changed the subject. Thea was working long hours on her textbook, and spending much of that time at the school library. So Cady waited, looking for a sign from her, anything to show she intended to sit down and have it out with him. He had his own embarrassment about Mr. Lowell, too, never having told Thea about his trips out to his cabin.

As if it were planned to keep Cady and Thea apart, Velda and Pete came over almost every day. Pete brought his new Scrabble game, and Velda brought cookies for Thea to taste and judge. Pete said Velda was working hard to show Ingvald how well she could cook, in case he might let her stay.

In the middle of the week, when it had quit snowing, Pete and Cady went out to the pond and cleared off the snow so they could skate. But before Thea would let them, she put on her skates and skated across the pond several times. Then she circled the ice once more, skating backward. Her long legs were as graceful as a dancer's. She was laughing and puffing when she sat down to take off her skates. "I had to see if it was safe," she said, halfway apologetic to the three waiting children.

She suggested they build a fire first, before they skated. They all gathered wood and stacked it nearby. Cady was using Thea's skates, and Pete had Ingvald's. Velda was going to take turns with Cady, because Ingvald's were much too large for her. Thea sat on a log near the fire and watched as they laced up their shoes. Her eyes rested on Cady. "You know my brother almost drowned. He went through the ice on our pond at home. He saved himself, like you did in the creek, Cady." She stirred the fire, causing sparks to fly. She studied Cady's face for a moment before turning away.

They skated every day after that, Velda flying in her red coat, like something exploding on ice. She hadn't skated often, she told Cady, but she was a natural. She sang as she skated, and the happiness on her face was so fragile it hurt Cady to look at her.

One day while she was taking off her skates, she said, "I really hope they have a rotten time." Her small face tightened up into a scowl.

"Who?" Cady asked.

She looked at him, surprised. "My mom and her boyfriend. Who else?"

"Why?"

"They don't deserve a good time."

"Why?"

123

"Is that all you can say is who-who-who, or why-why-why?"

"If that's the way you feel, I don't think I care." Cady took the skates from her, and he turned his back to put them on.

"Because of the way she treats us kids." She yelled it in his ear. "And the way she treats DeDe better than us. She's crazy about him. I don't think he's really our brother. I think maybe he doesn't belong to our dad."

Pete had skated back in time to hear what she had said. "You're saying something crazy," he said. But his mouth was drawn down, and his eyes unsteady. "She always blamed me because he went away. The things I did, getting into trouble."

"Don't shoot yourself down, Pete. Mom gives me a pain. She doesn't think about anybody but herself." Velda ran and slid a few feet on the ice. When she came back, her face was softer. "It's just that she and her boyfriend are going up to Little Falls to get married today. Ingvald said he got a letter. And he looked real sour when he told me."

"It's too bad you couldn't have gone," Cady said.

"I wouldn't have—if they had asked me." Velda sniffed hard and gagged on her tears.

"It just goes to prove that some people change— keep changing. You're always on the outside." Cady thought of Thea. She didn't change, but there was a wall between them.

Cady took off his skates sooner than he had wanted to and gave them to Velda. He watched her when she started to skate. The contented look came back to her eyes, and she began to dance on the ice again. The sun had disappeared behind the huge jack pines, and Pete's and Velda's voices were magnified in the cold air. Cady thought of Thea avoiding him since Christmas and not wanting to explain about Mr. Lowell, of all the pretending and covering up. He felt like he was dangling in space, and no one was reaching out to pull him in—neither Thea nor Mr. Lowell.

Thea planned a supper at the cave on New Year's Eve. Pete and Velda were invited to spend the night with Cady. At ten o'clock they started for the cave. Each one of them carried a basket of food. It was cold, and it took a huge fire at the mouth of the cave to keep warm.

"You must have Gypsy blood," Thea said, watching Cady make the fire.

"Why do you say that?" He became alert. Lately Cady was always waiting for Thea to let slip some of the things he wanted to know.

"The way you can build a fire." She smiled at him. "And the way you like to be here alone in your cave like an old hermit."

"I don't mind being alone. I could live here."

"I could, too, I guess. It's in my blood, at least when I was a kid." Thea laughed. "I guess I have a primitive urge to be close to the earth—to live near the birds and the beasts."

Cady looked expectantly at Thea. "I'm like that, too. I've got that urge."

Thea nodded, pleased. "I really like the simple things—bathe in the sea, and dress in reeds." She paused, laughing at herself again. "Forget the meddlesome world and the meddlesome people."

"I'd like to forget them, too," Velda agreed. She

and Pete sat huddled together, wrapped in a blanket. Velda kept feeding the fire, more than was needed. At last she said what was on her mind. "I don't think Uncle Ingvald should let me go home. If he doesn't want me, I could live in this cave. I wouldn't be afraid."

"Oh, but you would get cold." Thea shivered.

"We haven't heard from her," Pete said.

"The 'her' being your mother?" Thea looked across at Pete. When she caught his eyes, she smiled.

"Not one word," Velda continued. "She's just gone off on her honeymoon. She doesn't want bratty kids around. We'd spoil the picture." When Velda laughed, it wasn't happy. She yanked her hood down, shadowing her face, and rested her chin in her hands.

When the coals were red, Thea put foil-wrapped potatoes in the fire. After opening it, she put a huge can of beans on the fire. She unscrewed the lid on the thermos, and poured them hot cocoa in paper cups. They became quiet, watching the fire with their own thoughts.

"If you lived like this out here in the woods, no one would know about you, would they?" Cady said suddenly to Thea. "You could just vanish. If somebody was looking for you, they'd never find you."

"I guess you could vanish if you wanted to. At least you'd learn how to survive alone." She stirred the fire, her face turned away from Cady. "The wisest have always lived a more simple and meager life, forgetting the luxuries and comforts. . . . I think Thoreau said that."

She sounded like Mr. Lowell. "Where do we fit in? Are we the wisest?" Cady asked.

Thea thought for a minute. "We may be—then on

the other hand, we may be the poorest, too." She laughed.

"Then that is the reason you and I live out here together, because we are wise and poor. And that's the reason for anyone to live out here?" Cady hadn't intended to sound funny, but he heard Pete and Velda snickering. He was more interested in prodding Thea to answer his questions.

"One of the reasons." She leaned over and turned the potatoes.

"What are the other reasons?" Cady's eyes were veiled and he was excited.

"Of course, being poor was the clincher," Thea said. "But not the main reason. I like it here. It's my home now. It's where my roots are. And I like the solitude. I want to work on more books."

"I'd have to have someone close, at least one person," Velda said softly. "You, Pete." She nudged him.

"Not me," Cady said.

"Are you sure?" Thea turned around to look at him, surprised. Cady saw a strange twist to her mouth. Then she shook her head impatiently. "Sometimes we don't know what we want."

When they began to smell the potatoes burning, Thea pushed them to the edge of the fire and they roasted wieners. With her heavy mittens, she grabbed at the beans boiling away. They sat close together, halfway back in the cave with just their feet sticking out while they ate.

Pete stopped eating long enough to tell them a story he'd read in the paper about two guys who had started, as young boys, spending every New Year's together. They went out to the woods and took a tent. At exactly midnight, standing out there in the middle of all those trees, where it was peaceful and quiet, they shouted "Happy New Year" to the whole world. "That's neat, really neat," Pete said. "Let's do it."

"Like you could make everybody in the world happy," Velda said.

"We could try," Thea said.

At a minute to midnight, by Thea's watch, they unscrambled from their blankets, and standing in a circle with their arms around each other they screamed, "Happy New Year." When it was suddenly quiet, Cady had a prickly sensation. He felt, for sure, that somewhere in the dark, where he couldn't be seen, Mr. Lowell was watching them.

"Look up there." Thea nudged Cady. "If you watch carefully, you can see the old year moving out." Giggling, they all stared at the sky. "Now watch, it'll move just like a shadow across the stars." They hadn't let go of each other. The stars did seem fainter and farther away to Cady.

"Oh, crazy!" Velda said, but still she stared up at the sky. She, like Cady, wanted to believe it.

"I used to think that," Cady said in her ear.

"That's nuts," Pete said.

A bell was ringing somewhere. In the distance they heard the sharp sound of a gun. Closer, Cady heard a bark. Then it was silent. And Cady felt the presence of two ghostly figures—the one stalking across the sky, and the other nearby, hiding in the trees.

19

The first week of January it snowed every day, and the temperature went down to below zero. Cady got used to his cold room, jumping out of bed and pulling on his pants, and carrying the rest of his clothes down to the kitchen.

The school bus couldn't make it through the drifts. In the mornings Cady walked the half mile to get their mail, and later filled the wood box and loaded the back porch with as much wood as it would hold. Thea kept the oven running, baking bread and most of their dinners. "Anything," she said, "to have a reason to keep the oven going." They lighted the fireplace early in the afternoon, and it burned until late at night. Sometimes when Thea was tired of working at the typewriter, they put up a card table and played gin rummy and double solitaire in front of the fire. Once in a while Thea mentioned Mr. Lowell, to say, "He has plenty of wood stored. He won't get cold. He has company, the fox. He has food to last the winter."

Cady thought she tried to sound impersonal.

"You do shop for him?" he asked.

"Yes, I have."

"He doesn't come here much?"

"No." She didn't invite Cady to ask more questions.

Velda had not gone home. Her mother ignored her letters. "She must still be on her totally awesome honeymoon," Velda said. Pete was happy, and Ingvald was on edge. He confided to Thea that Velda had come with very few clothes, not even enough for a week. Thea gave her one of her nightgowns and some underwear. She took one of her skirts in at the side seams and shortened it for Velda. Pete walked over a couple of times. Thea sent a sweater home with him that she said was too small. He said Velda couldn't come, she was so busy cleaning house for Ingvald. She was doing drawers and closets, and Ingvald was having a fit because she was throwing so much away. Pete laughed hard, his mouth spread wide, when he told about Velda baking pie and cake and some awful bread that was too hard to chew. "Don't laugh at her," Thea said to him. "You know why. She's begging to stay."

The day the sun came out it was a blinding sea of white, the drifts frozen into waves and curlicues, impossible to walk through. Thea found an old pair of snowshoes in the barn and showed Cady how to use them. Cady tried them around the yard, at first awkward and falling down. Then he got the hang of it, pointing his feet out and sliding. After days of practice he went as far as the pond. The drifts were huge. He managed most of the time to stay on top. Each day he went farther, and his legs felt less strained.

On the next Saturday he decided to try and get as far as Mr. Lowell's cabin. First he went to his room and took the carved bird off his chest. He put it in the pocket of his coat so Thea wouldn't notice. The mile to the cabin seemed like ten to Cady. When he was still quite a way from the log house, he was glad to see the smoke rising from it. But when he came in sight of it, he lost some of his courage. He went toward it as quietly as possible and crept up to the window. Even though he was ashamed of spying, he peeked in.

Mr. Lowell was sitting in his big chair reading, the fox at his feet, its head resting up against the man's leg. There was nothing frightening about Mr. Lowell. His face was relaxed, pleasant. He looked younger, more like Thea. Cady stood for minutes watching the man. From outside the window he was able to feel comfortable with him. Catching him this way, he thought maybe they could talk to each other.

With this in mind, Cady knocked boldly on the door. He was pleased to see he had startled Mr. Lowell, so much so he invited Cady in without hesitation. He looked down as Cady took off his snowshoes, and smiled as if forgetting himself. "Can you manage those things? I never could."

"How do you get around in the snow, then?" Cady asked.

"I don't." He took Cady's jacket and threw it onto one of the bunks. He sat down in his chair and motioned for Cady to pull a bench up to the fire. Then it was quiet again. The fox laid his head back against the man's leg. They both stared at Cady. Mr. Lowell's face changed. It was tense and suspicious.

"Do you know where the cave is, by the pond?" Cady asked.

"Should I?"

Cady shook his head quickly. "No, maybe not." He put his hand out to the fox. The fox did not move his head from Mr. Lowell's shin, his fluid eyes on Cady. "It's hard to find. I don't know how I came to stumble on it. You can hardly tell it's there." He turned all of his attention to Mr. Lowell now. "I had to cut down a little pine so I could get in easier. I can see the pond from there, and sometimes the ducks come out on it. They did this fall. I've seen a deer, too."

"Did you, now."

"In the summer there are a lot of thimbleberries out in front, and one day a whole flock of cedar waxwings came down and spent an hour eating. . . . I'll show you sometime." Cady paused.

"Why did you come?" Mr. Lowell's voice was quiet, just above a whisper.

Cady went on as if he hadn't been interrupted. "The cave is mine. I own it. Thea said so."

"Don't claim anything. That's the best way to lose it." Mr. Lowell got up quickly, went outside and brought back a load of wood in his arms. He threw a large log on the fire that started a crackling, and flames shooting up the chimney.

"We built a fire at the mouth of my cave and it keeps us warm no matter how cold. We were out there New Year's Eve." Cady looked quickly at Mr. Lowell. "We had a supper, then we wished a Happy New Year to anybody around here that might hear us. Could you hear it back this far?"

"How would I hear it?"

"If you were listening, you might."

The man put his head down. He ran his finger down the fox's nose.

"If you were listening, you could have heard it." Cady repeated. "Were you there, too? I thought maybe you were, because I heard Reynard bark."

When Mr. Lowell looked up at him, his eyes were a fierce blue. "Why did you come?"

Cady couldn't think for a moment. His mouth felt puckered and unmovable, his lips stiff. Then he remembered the carved bird in the pocket of his coat. He walked over to the bunk and slipped his hand into the pocket around the carved bird. When he brought it out, his hand was trembling. He held it out to Mr. Lowell.

"You forgot your present. I brought it to you," Cady said.

"You expect me to thank you?"

"You don't have to." Cady pushed the bird at him. "Don't you want it?"

Mr. Lowell looked from Cady's face to his hand; then his eyes slid away to the fox at his feet. "I left it, didn't I?"

The wind was blowing, and the sound of it outside in the pines made a strange howling that filled Cady's head. He looked for some gentleness in the man's face, for some recognition of himself. He noticed that when Mr. Lowell looked at the fox there was a melting in his eyes, a warmth that surged upward into his face, flushing it. It made Cady angry. He reached out suddenly and placed the bird in the man's hand and he held it there. "I won't take it back with me. It's yours. Keep it!"

He grabbed his jacket and snowshoes, and buttoned up on the way to the door. He didn't stop to
put on the snowshoes, but waded through the snow
with them under his arm until he was out of sight of
the cabin.

20

Pete and Velda finally heard from their mother. She sent Velda her school grades with the message that she was moving to Austin, and she would write when she had a place for them. Cady was surprised when he found out that Velda was going into the ninth grade, ahead of him. Thea went with Ingvald to register her at school. She was to start the next Monday at the beginning of the semester.

Ingvald gave Thea a long list of clothes to buy for Velda. They all went into town together, but Ingvald sat in the tavern and drank coffee while he waited. Velda went from terribly happy to embarrassed. Cady could see that she didn't like anyone to have to do things for her. Thea knew a lot more about picking out girls' clothes than she did boys', but she and Velda asked Cady's opinion about everything they bought. He thought it was because Thea didn't want him to be jealous. They settled on two skirts, a pair of jeans and two sweaters. The last thing they bought was a red coat with pile lining and a hood, which she wore out of the store. When they got back to the tavern, Ingvald insisted on treating them to fried chicken and coleslaw. They all crowded into a booth, and Cady sat between Pete and Velda. He had never had friends before, not like this.

The next day Cady and Thea went over to Ingvald's to help fix a room for Velda in the attic. A door off the front room led up to it. The stairway was cold, and the room had slanting ceilings and small windows. A chimney ran through the corner of the room. A single bed and an old chest of drawers were the only furniture. Thea put the boys to work wiping down the walls and washing the woodwork and floor. She insisted on two coats of wax, and Velda polished. Cady and Pete carried the mattress out to air. When Thea went home in the afternoon, she found curtains and several small throw rugs she had stored away.

Later, when they had finished, while they were drinking tea and eating cheese sandwiches, Cady looked around at all of them. Thea was at the center, her face smudged and tired. Velda, her face creased in happiness, sat close to her, as if this were the most natural thing in the world—a family circle. It was Thea who made it that way, Cady thought. She could turn things around, pounding cement into cracks so nothing could fall apart. But still she wasn't willing to talk to him, to tell him where he fit in.

He turned it over and over in his mind, and by the time they got home he was so full of questions he thought he'd explode. He went into the kitchen where Thea was drinking coffee. He carried the watch she had given him.

"Was this your dad's watch?"

"Yes, I told you that."

"How about those pictures up there in my room, that man and that woman. Is that your dad and mother?"

"No, that's my grandfather and grandmother. This was their farm, and my dad grew up here. I've told you this before." Thea looked at him, puzzled.

Cady teetered on his toes, then rocked back on his heels. "Why did you give the watch to me?"

"Because I wanted to." Thea's eyes opened wide.

"No special reason?"

"Probably a lot of special reasons I don't have time to list."

"Just name one."

Thea turned her head impatiently. "Because I like you. Isn't that reason enough?"

"Why did you have to tell him all about me? You said I shouldn't talk about living in Missouri, and coming out of that creek alive—everybody down there thinks I'm drowned."

"Who are you talking about now?" She jumped up from the table and dumped her cup in the sink and rinsed it. When she closed the cupboard doors, she banged them.

"Mr. Lowell."

"Let's not talk about it tonight, Cady, I'm tired." She reached to turn out the light.

"I went to see him." Thea nodded her head. "He called himself Thoreau. I'd just like to know what his real name is," Cady said.

"Well, we know it isn't Thoreau." Thea sat down again. "He knows better than that," she said, shaking her head.

"He was trying to pull my leg?"

"I think he does that quite often."

"I think he plays a game."

"Could be."

"Does it make you mad?"

Thea hesitated. "No."

"It would me. Do you think if he keeps a record in the journal you gave him, he'll know who he is, Thoreau or Mr. Lowell?"

"That's not a joke."

"I'd just like to know what his problem is. Something must have turned him off."

"I guess you could say that."

"Kind of like, stop the world I want to get off?"

Thea nodded.

"He's alone, isn't he?"

"It's up to someone like me to help him, then, isn't it?"

"I guess so."

"It isn't healthy to turn your back on the world entirely. It's one way of ending your life."

"Is that what he's trying to do?"

"No more tonight." Thea rubbed her head as if it hurt.

Cady started out the door, then he turned. "I feel sorry for him—that he's got this problem."

"That's good of you." Thea puzzled over this. "I don't know whether Mr. Lowell would want that or not, want anyone to feel sorry for him and his problem." She pressed her hand to her mouth in an absentminded way. "Once he wouldn't have. He was very independent." Her eyes drifted across Cady's face. She spoke again in an odd voice. "No, I don't think he would want either one of us to feel sorry for him—not that from us."

Cady felt shadows in the room—something from the past that clouded their lives. When he went upstairs, he opened the small window at the foot of his bed a crack. It had started to snow and blow. He was glad for the old couple in the painting on the wall. He rolled up in his blankets, his head near the window. The disturbing wind came in great gusts, shaking the house at times. Toward morning the wind died, and it was peaceful again. Cady was able to sleep then.

21

On Monday when Cady got on the bus, Velda motioned for him to sit with her. Pete was in the seat behind her, with his chin resting on the back, talking in her ear. Cady couldn't help notice how nervous Velda was. She kept reaching under her coat to pat her armpits to see if she was dry.

"Anyone as smart as you doesn't need to worry about looks," Cady said.

"Says who?" Velda unbuttoned her coat and looked down at her sweater.

"You don't need to be scared and nervous. You've got Pete and me."

That made Velda giggle.

"What's so funny?"

"I usually need to look after Pete." She pressed her skirt pleats, one over the other, across her knees, and tucked her scuffy boots under the seat.

Cady felt genuinely sorry for her when they left

her at her homeroom door. She looked so little and skinny. But when Cady met her in the hall later, she flipped past him as if she didn't know him. She treated Pete the same way.

"Why did you have to act so stuck up today?" Pete asked her as they got on the bus.

"Yah, you were a little strange," Cady said.

She slid over near the window. She looked thoughtful for a moment. Then she pulled her hood down over her hair and across her brows, and tied it. "You don't know much about human nature," she said. "If you did you wouldn't always be worrying about what someone thinks about you. I don't."

Cady didn't believe her. He laughed. "That's why you put on such a good act, like, Velda's cool—nothing bothers her. Just get out of her way when she sweeps down the hall."

She stared at Cady as if he were a mealybug she'd like to step on. "You know that isn't true. You have to have intuitive powers to get by in this world." She leaned over and knocked the snow off her boot. "Right now I'm deciding who's going to be my friends, and who isn't. And I don't want you two to do anything to embarrass me." Cady and Pete about fell off the seat laughing.

But it was true. In just a few days Velda had friends—any number of kids around her. Cady would see them coming down the hall, all laughing, and she in the center, and the kids just lapping up what she was telling them. She tossed her head at Cady and gave him a smug "I told you so" look.

For a week it was bitter cold, and Cady didn't go out unless he had to. Thea drove him to the school bus. He spent the long evenings huddled in front of the fire while Thea worked on her manuscript. She gave him no chance to talk about Mr. Lowell.

The last week of January it warmed up. The ice melted and dripped from the roof, and the snow began to shrink into the earth. He went out to his cave to see if anyone had disturbed his things. It was the same as he had left it. He wasn't interested in building a fire and sitting around alone today. He started up the cliff behind the cave. He walked near where he had found Reynard in the trap.

Cady saw tracks coming from the opposite direction and returning the same way. He walked carefully to where the tracks stopped, and he noticed that the snow was messed up where someone had kicked it into a mound. He found a stick, and getting down on his knees he began to prod in the snow, reaching deeper until the stick was more than a foot in the snow, almost buried. Then he heard it, the savage sound of the trap closing on the stick. It was like a gunshot, and it affected Cady the same way—he whirled away from the hole as if he had been shot. He hadn't believed there would be a trap. The next minute he was so mad he started beating the snow with another stick, digging around until he uncovered the trap. He tried to remove it, but it was chained tightly to a rod that had been sunk into the ground and frozen in.

He was wet and cold. He took off running toward the log house, and he didn't care what Mr. Lowell said when he saw him. As he came closer to the house, some of the air went out of Cady and he slowed down. After knocking, he waited a few minutes and no one came. He felt like he was freezing to death, and he was greatly relieved when the door opened. Mr. Lowell stood there, rubbing his face. He gave every sign of having been asleep, including a disgruntled look. His eyes had hollows deep enough for Cady to bury his fist in.

"You," he said.

"I'm Cady," he said, as if trying to jog Mr. Lowell's memory. His teeth started to chatter so hard he couldn't say another word.

The man grabbed him by the elbow and marched him over to the fire. He started stripping off Cady's wet coat and pants, and threw him a robe. After he drank the hot coffee that Mr. Lowell brought him, and had quit shaking, Cady said, "You don't have to ask me why I came. I'll tell you."

Mr. Lowell sat down opposite him. The fox moved against his leg, and he put his hand on its head. "Don't talk yet. Just get warmed up," he said.

Cady stared at the fox. "He doesn't have a splint on. He must be healed." The man nodded. "I'm glad for that. I went back up on the ridge today, and I found another trap, the same place I found Reynard in the trap. I thought maybe there wouldn't be any more after I found that other one. I thought you'd want to know. Do you?" Cady looked up at the man. He thought he saw respect in the man's eyes. "I tried to get the trap out of the hole, but I couldn't. You should go get it. I got it tripped so it can't hurt anything. Every one I find I'm going to smash!"

"That's a good idea." The man swiveled back and forth in his chair.

"I told you before, I don't do it for you. I do it for the fox." Cady squirmed around on the bench so he wasn't looking so directly at Mr. Lowell. "I think everything should have a fair deal, a chance. I don't like killing."

"Neither do I."

Cady reached out to the fox, and rubbed him on the head. "I know you like him a lot."

"Then you did it for me, too, didn't you?" The mockery was there again in his eyes. He didn't give Cady a chance to answer, but got up quickly and left the room. When he came back, he had a sandwich for Cady.

"Why did you tell me that you were Thoreau, and why do you live out here like this?" Cady waited until the man sat down again to continue. "It must be lonely. If you didn't have the fox, it would be."

"Everyone in the world is alone—lonely—at times. Neither God nor man can prevent that."

"Don't you have anyone—a family?"

"Why do you ask me such questions?"

"People have to claim someone."

"You think so?"

"What else is there to expect? Don't you have anyone to claim—I mean for your own?" Cady's eyes never wavered from Mr. Lowell's face.

"Do you?" Mr. Lowell lowered his head, rubbing the fox's neck with both his hands.

Cady took a big bite of his sandwich and chewed it for as long as he could make it last. He was thinking. This would be a time to answer with a half truth that would be more true than the whole truth. "Yes,"

144

he said. He didn't explain he was speaking of Thea.

"Can you claim someone who is dead?" Mr. Lowell's eyes were a fierce blue.

"It would depend."

"On what?"

"On how much you loved them." Cady's tongue seemed to thicken and stumble over the words.

"That doesn't bring them back."

"In a way it could." Cady felt he'd gotten in over his head. His heart was thumping faster than it should. He was afraid to look down at his chest for fear the thumping would show through his T-shirt. "You must have somebody." The silence pressed against Cady and made him cold. He started shivering again. He waited as long as he could stand it, then he crawled over to the fox and touched him to feel his warmth. "I know I want to have something of my own, somewhere I belong, that will be that way for the rest of my life." His face was against the fox's neck. Cady wasn't sure Mr. Lowell heard him. "That's the way I'm going to have it," he said.

"Thea seems to be doing that for you." Mr. Lowell rose so fast his chair fell over. He brought out a pair of pants and a heavy jacket and tossed them to Cady. Cady had to roll the pants up and the jacket came to his knees.

They went out together to look for the trap. The thawing made rivers of slush, and the jack pines seemed to drip green rain. Neither spoke as they walked side by side. When they found the trap they smashed it out of shape so it could not be used again. Mr. Lowell went as far as the cave with Cady. When Cady walked on, he looked back to see Mr. Lowell standing still, watching after him.

As he undressed for bed that night, Cady looked up at the old couple in the frame. "I'll have it my way," he said to them. "I'll make him notice me." He threw his shoe and hit the wall.

22

It came to Cady gradually, and it was something that he didn't like to think about, but he looked forward more and more to seeing Velda on the bus, or bumping into her in the halls. She usually had her friends with her. He felt tongue-tied and awkward when he talked to her, and it was hard for him to look directly at her. But he liked to be around her. So when Cady first suggested that Pete help him start a science project to enter in the school Science Fair, he hoped that it might interest Velda, too.

Velda ignored it. It was Pete who got excited. He had half a dozen ideas, but they settled on the study of wildlife. In the school library they found books on plants and animals, and an illustrated manual of experiments. Cady also brought home *National Geographic, National Wildlife, Natural History,* and *The Conservationist.* Pete came home with Cady almost every night, and they read through the books and magazines, and learned how to discover animal homes, and how to identify animal tracks. Cady was especially interested in the diagrams for making a plaster-of-paris cast of tracks. Ingvald suggested they had better find an animal if they wanted to make a cast.

The first track was hard to find. Pete figured they could get chicken tracks out of the yard for a start. Cady explained that wouldn't be too unusual, and they weren't wild. On the next Saturday they went out looking for a rabbit burrow or a beaver lodge near the pond. There were no burrows or lodges to be seen in the snow. They found beaver and deer tracks in the snow, but the few tracks they did find frozen in the mud softened and lost shape before they could set the plaster of paris.

The thought hit Cady so suddenly he was surprised he hadn't come up with it before. The fox. He could make a cast of the fox's tracks and study his habits. He would get Mr. Lowell to help him. They could work together, and it might please the man that Cady had chosen Reynard for his project, and he could explain how Mr. Lowell had tamed the fox. And it would give Cady an excuse to go out to his house.

Pete went with him. They carried a notebook and the materials for making casts in a shopping bag. When Mr. Lowell opened the door, he said, "You're back." It sounded to Cady as though he sighed. He motioned for Pete and Cady to come in. "Did you find another trap?" he asked.

"No." Cady felt awkward now. "We're doing a science project about wildlife. We've been trying to find a burrow, or a den, and study the animal in it."

"Yes."

"It's the wrong time of year. Everything is covered

with snow. We can't find any animals," Cady said.

"You might have thought of that first."

"What about Reynard? If we could make some track casts—and write a paper about his habits. You could tell us all about taming him." Cady talked fast before the man could say no.

"That's really why you came?" The man's eyes had darkened.

"I wanted to come, or I wouldn't have," Cady said. For the first time he noticed the fox was not in the room. "Where is he?"

Mr. Lowell pointed out the window. When Cady looked he saw the run, about ten feet long and three feet wide. The fox was trotting from one end to the other. "I put him out there to exercise. I've never had to shut him up before."

"Because of the trap?"

"Because of the trapper. I have always let Reynard have the same privileges as I had, to do as he pleased."

"Does he mind?"

"Wouldn't you? But he's not there long. He's in the house most of the time with me."

Pete, standing between them, seemed to make it more comfortable for both Cady and Mr. Lowell. "I thought if we could study the fox's habits, learn more about him and describe him in detail—how you tamed him—well, we'd have a fox to look at, and somebody who knew a lot about them."

"You mean me?" Mr. Lowell asked.

"You probably know more about a fox than anyone else."

Then Pete started asking questions about how Mr. Lowell had found the fox, and how he had made a pet out of it. Cady answered before Mr. Lowell could. "He lives alone. He's got no one else. The fox is good company." Cady saw the man's eyes quicken, as if he were about to say something. Instead he started for the back door.

"I suppose you'd like to see him." He came back in a minute with the fox running at his heel like a dog. Pete backed off at first until Cady showed him how to approach the fox, to let the fox sniff him.

"How are you going to start? I see you brought all of your paraphernalia with you." Mr. Lowell watched, a skeptical look on his face, as Cady began to empty the bag on the floor. He pulled out a small wooden box, a pan and a bag of soil. He asked Mr. Lowell for a cup of water that he mixed with the soil to a thick mud, spreading it thinly in the box. It took a while to convince Reynard that he should put his foot in the box, and Mr. Lowell had to help. It took two times to get a good track. Cady let it set near the fire for a few minutes while he mixed the plaster of paris. He sprinkled talcum powder into the footprint, and then poured the plaster of paris, thick as heavy cream, into the box. Cady didn't talk while he worked. He could feel Mr. Lowell's eyes on him. Pete lay on his stomach in front of the fire with the notebook in front of him. He asked Mr. Lowell more questions and laboriously took notes.

While the cast dried, Cady looked at the books on the shelves, reading the titles. He picked up two books, *The Lord of the Flies* and *The Catcher in the Rye,* and looked at the inscriptions. In one he read: "Good reading. Merry Christmas! to my brother, 1965." Cady was embarrassed to find Mr. Lowell watching him.

"Were you looking for anything in particular?" he asked.

Cady looked at several more books before he turned around. He felt sure now his face would not give him away. "I've read a lot of these myself." he said.

"Mine, when I was a kid." Mr. Lowell went out to his small kitchen and made a pot of coffee and beef sandwiches. Later he helped Cady take the mold from the box and wash off the mud. But he had become watchful and silent again.

Before they left, Cady offered him the fox's footprint, so perfectly held in the plaster of paris. "I thought you'd like to have this to remember him by, so you won't ever forget him." He saw the quick anger come into the man's eyes, and he was sorry. "I'll keep it if you want it later," Cady said. "Anyway, we'll make more of them."

Walking home, Pete complained about Mr. Lowell. "He's weird. I don't think he likes kids," he said.

"Oh yes he does. It's just he's afraid of them," Cady said.

Pete's mouth stretched wide, and he laughed loudly at the idea. But Cady was certain of this now. He might have added, "I think it's me he's afraid of."

23

On the first warm Saturday in February, Pete and Velda came over and walked with Cady. First they went to the pond, and then because it was so chilly they went on to the cave. The boys built a fire, and Velda watched from the mouth of the cave. Cady noticed her face looked kind of peaked and sad.

"She's thinking she should go home," Pete volunteered.

"Why should she?"

"Oh, Ingvald is mad at her. He got called to school because she talks too much. And some of the kids have been writing things on the bathroom walls about her. And she's boy crazy, Ingvald says."

"Too bad for him." Velda had leaned forward to hear what they were saying. "None of it is true, and the only girl writing rotten things about me is jealous. And Ma says that's what makes the world go round, is boyfriends."

"Look at all the trouble it got your ma into," Cady said.

"What trouble?" Velda hunched herself forward, her elbows on her knees.

"Getting married all the time—and not keeping her kids."

"So what."

"I'd think you'd want to try to stay here." Cady squatted down near her.

"I really don't care where I am. Ingvald is mad at me, and she is mad at me most of the time. And everybody acts like it's such a hassle to have me around. I'd just as soon die."

Pete shrugged. "She's nuts when she gets this way."

"Do you want me to stay?" Velda looked up at Cady. "What I mean is, you're not part of my family, or anyone that should care one way or the other. But would it make any difference to you?"

Cady thought it was about the silliest question he had ever heard, because of course he'd care if she left. She should know it. But when he looked down at her, she was staring into the fire like she was trying to read her whole future, and she was off alone by herself.

"Did you know there are a lot of older people who love each other more than they do their kids?" Velda's eyes grew misty. She laid her cheek on her knee. "They even forget they have kids around, and the kids have got feelings. I've seen it happen all the time. It's sickening, just one long love affair. That's the way it is with my mom and her boyfriends. I'm never going to have kids." Her freckles stood out on her pale face, and her eyes were puffy from crying. "I had a formal weaning—real early."

"Me, too." Cady tried to laugh.

"Does it make a difference to you what I do?" Velda's eyes were questioning, and the pain that came so easily hung around her mouth. "All I want to know is, does it matter to anyone what I do?" She kicked angrily at a half-burned log that had rolled out of the fire. "I'd just like to know where I stand."

"It sure makes a difference with me. I'd be crazy if it didn't." Cady sat down beside her. "I think you should stay."

"Anyway, we can depend on Ingvald. Maybe he's mad at you, Velda, but he won't kick us out—I know," Pete said.

Cady thought about depending on Thea, and about the old house that was home for them. The fire flared in a sudden gust, and the warmth curled up inside him, matching the bright flame. "You need people to feel safe," he said. "You can't go it alone." It was the first time he had been willing to admit it. "I don't think I'd want to go away." He spoke slowly. "Not now."

So while Velda talked of her problems, Cady listened carefully, trying to give her the right answers and to be honest. Later Cady patiently explained the science project to her, and how she could help them. She didn't agree until Pete began to hop around the fire, yelling that she could do the posters and draw sketches of the fox that would make it walk right off the paper.

The next time Cady and Pete went to the man's house they took Velda. She brought a sketch pad and a charcoal pencil. She didn't shy from the fox, but went right up to it—like one wild animal to another, Cady thought. If Mr. Lowell was surprised to see the three of them, he didn't show it. Velda was not afraid or nervous with Mr. Lowell. "I'd like to draw your fox," she said.

"Do you know how?" Mr. Lowell looked down from a height that might have scared most kids.

"I'm here" was her quick reply. She pointed to her sketch pad. She looked him straight in the eye. It bothered Cady that she seemed better able to handle the man than he was. "Does he sit still long?" she asked.

"That's up to you. An animal knows when you have control."

"I'll have control. I'll show him what I'm trying to draw. He'll recognize himself." She sat down on the floor cross-legged, unbuttoning her coat and letting it fall to the floor. Velda shook her hair out of her face and sat staring at the fox, who had not moved and who stared back. "I can't put in your color, not today. I brought only my charcoal. Later I'll make you wheat and gold color."

"No," Cady said, "More bronze than gold."

"His nose is smudged." Velda had started to draw. "So are his ears and legs."

"His coat is rust, not bronze." Mr. Lowell spoke quietly. "He has white, too, on the tip of his tail."

"He looks as if he wore a mask." Velda continued, as if she had not been interrupted.

"And his eyes are yellow, almost gold, like a peeled grape. They are like looking deep into a pool," Cady said.

Mr. Lowell sat down in his chair near Velda, and

Pete watched over her shoulder. As the sketch progressed, Cady thought he could almost see what she had added by watching Pete's face. When he began to grin and look pleased, Cady was certain it was near done.

But when Cady saw it, he wasn't satisfied. "He should be moving. He's very graceful. When he whirls and leaps he looks as if he's dancing. The first time I saw him . . ." Cady stopped talking. He thought of the day the fox had led him here. He looked up at Mr. Lowell. "He took my breath the first time I saw him."

Mr. Lowell nodded. "An animal is beautiful in its natural setting—when it's not fearful."

"What makes it fearful?" Velda asked.

"To be hounded." Mr. Lowell bit out the words.

"But it's not in its natural setting here," Cady said.

"I didn't expect this when I brought him home. I expected him to return to the wild. As soon as I thought he was able to take care of himself, I let him run. But he always returned to me." Mr. Lowell sounded defensive.

"He wanted to be close to you," Cady said.

"I guess you could say so." There was sadness in Mr. Lowell's face when he spoke.

Velda had stopped drawing. She tore out the sheet and handed it to Mr. Lowell. "Could you guess it was a fox?"

"I think you could." He studied the page. "I think it would be better if the fox was moving, as Cady suggested, to show its beauty."

"Sure would. I never saw one sitting before," Pete said.

"You never saw one before, period." Cady said.

"Who says so?"

"You told me yourself."

"Well, anyway, they shouldn't be standing still."

"I will next time. I'll do it several ways. And I'll do a few in color, using my crayons." Velda shrugged her shoulders as if there were nothing to it. She scrambled to her feet, shaking out her sweater and hiking up her heavy pants. Cady noticed she moved with the magic grace of an elf, and as playfully as one, when she took a quick step to the fox, leaned over it and kissed it on the top of its head, between the ears. She was unafraid and the fox was unafraid. It licked her hand, and Mr. Lowell laughed suddenly. Cady strained to hear the laugh, memorizing the sound until it folded into silence. If I could make him laugh, he thought.

Going home later, Velda ran on ahead. "If we run we won't get cold," she said. She danced instead of walking. Her shadow was like a moth, fluttering and drooping. Cady caught up with her and put his arm across her shoulders. He wanted to share the closeness that she had with Mr. Lowell.

24

They went regularly to Mr. Lowell's now. Sometimes
Velda sketched, other times she played with the fox.
Mr. Lowell treated the three of them alike. He listened to their chatter, and Velda's laughter overflow-
ing, rarely speaking himself. Some days he popped
corn and set the bowl on the floor beside them. One
afternoon he dug out a cribbage board and taught
them to play.

At times Cady resented the attention that Velda
was able to draw from Mr. Lowell. It was Cady's idea,
his project. Now he wished he didn't have to share
it. But he wouldn't have dared to come so often if it
hadn't been for Velda. She said it was good for Mr.
Lowell, that he was a lonely man, not like Ingvald,
who seemed never to be lonely or unhappy. When
Mr. Lowell was distant, she acted as if she didn't notice. Sometimes Cady felt like turning and running,
the man was so changeable.

On the days they could get Mr. Lowell to talk, they

asked him all sorts of questions, and recorded in detail all the information about Reynard. Velda made sketches of Reynard growing from a tiny kit to full grown, as the man described him.

Thea had never come with them. One night she walked to meet them. She said she was interested in what they were doing and asked about the project. Later, when they were eating supper, Cady tried to talk to her about Mr. Lowell.

"Why doesn't Mr. Lowell live here?"

"Why would he live here?" Her words came very carefully.

"Velda says he's lonely."

"Maybe Velda doesn't understand."

"I don't understand, either."

"He used to come to the house quite often. He doesn't now. Sometimes while you are at school I go to see him. I can't help the way things are."

"Who is he?"

"Mr. Lowell." Thea's eyes were steady.

"He doesn't come because of me?"

"That's some of it." She studied Cady for a moment. "I brought him here because he was a sick man. He was in the veterans' hospital." Suddenly her eyes grew warmer, flooded with concern that she had hurt Cady. She stared at him for a long time without speaking. When she did, her voice was flat. "I've known him a long time. I wish you would accept him the way he is."

"Will he accept me the way I am?" Cady asked. Thea didn't answer. She became stiff and unnatural, as if a door had closed, shutting her away from Cady. He was afraid to ask more.

159

The Science Fair was the eighteenth of March. Velda had made a cover for the diary with a sketch of the fox, and the title printed across the top: THE DIARY OF REYNARD, THE FOX. Cady and Pete had made several impressions of both the front and back feet of Reynard, and had arranged them across a beaver-board covered with green crepe paper. They had measured the length of his stride and the position of each foot as the fox trotted in the snow.

During this time, while they were visiting Mr. Low-ell almost every day, it seemed to Cady that as Mr. Lowell became more comfortable with Velda and Pete, he became more distant with him. He wondered, too, about Mr. Lowell's sickness, what it was. It didn't show, not anything Cady noticed.

A few days before the Science Fair, they took the completed diary and sketches over for Mr. Lowell to see. He took a long time to read through the diary, and nodded his head in approval. They each gave their talks that went with the exhibit. Mr. Lowell sat in his big chair by the fire.

Pete led off. He licked his lips, then wiped them carefully with the back of his hand. "The fox was imported to this country in 1650," he began. "It is a curious and intelligent animal, making it possible to train and to make a pet of one." Holding up her sketches, Velda described the physical strength and beauty of the fox. Cady watched the man's face as he listened. The fox sat between Mr. Lowell's feet, his head resting on the man's leg. It struck Cady that they had a kind of silent dignity that made them seem untouchable.

When it was Cady's turn, he spoke without using

his notes, directing all of his words to Mr. Lowell. He described seeing the fox for the first time, and its leading him to the man's cabin. Cady's face was flushed and he spoke slowly. He told of later finding the fox in the trap, injured. He finished by describing the loyalty of the male to its mate and kits. "It will stay with the trapped vixen, unwilling to save itself. A fox won't desert its young," he said. Cady's glance moved away from Mr. Lowell. "Reynard the fox has been made a pet." Cady paused. "He is Mr. Lowell's closest companion—probably closer than anything else in the world to him."

The man's hand slipped away from the fox's head. Cady noticed his eyes were suddenly a fierce blue, then seemed to lose power as if he found it hard to look into Cady's face.

Before he left, Cady asked Mr. Lowell if he was coming to the fair. The man looked at him briefly, then away from him. "I might," he said. "And I might not—depends."

Cady, Velda and Pete set up their exhibit the afternoon before the fair started. They outlined the beaverboard with pine branches, and made a snowy background with cotton batting for the display of the diary and sketches. Everything that Cady put in place was with the idea Mr. Lowell might see it, and approve—if he came. Cady was half sick thinking that he might not.

Twenty minutes before it started, a gang of kids surrounded them, mostly Velda's friends. Cady was relieved when he saw Bart, a head taller than the rest, giving him a thumbs-up sign, his big patient grin spread across his face. When the demonstrations started, there was a rush of more people to their exhibit. Velda hooked her arm through Cady's. She hung on tight for a minute, and he knew she was as scared as he was.

Cady's eyes searched through the crowd looking for Mr. Lowell. He saw Thea and Ingvald, then at the last moment Mr. Lowell slipped in the door. Cady began to breathe fast, and he felt beads of sweat on his face. When it was his turn, he stood at the side of the display and spoke from memory. His mouth trembled at first. His eyes wavered, then settled on Mr. Lowell.

In his mind he saw them that day in the woods, the solitary man and the dancing fox. He thought of the reason he had picked Reynard for his science project. He remembered how at Christmas he had felt somehow joined to this man. And he knew that this project was a gift to him, like the hand-carved bird. He wanted him to accept it. As he described the taming of the fox, the man moved closer to the front.

"Mr. Lowell is very understanding of animals and how to treat them, and the fox depends on him—I can see why," Cady said. "The fox makes him happy, too. That's important. In a way they claim each other. That's important, too."

Mr. Lowell stood in front of him now, close enough to touch. "Very good," he said softly, "very good." When he walked away, he turned once and looked back at Cady. There was surprise on his face; then he smiled.

Afterward Cady went into a darkened classroom and closed the door. He sat at a desk and laid his head in his arms. He began to laugh uncontrollably. He was sure Mr. Lowell had accepted his gift. He sat there several minutes before he wiped his eyes and went back to the booth.

They won honorable mention. The only one mad about it was Velda.

25

On Saturday morning Cady walked over to Ingvald's and asked Velda and Pete to go with him to Mr. Lowell's to give him the ribbon they had won.

"It definitely belongs to Mr. Lowell," Velda said.

"It belongs to Reynard, if I have my say-so," Pete said.

Cady knew that he wanted to give it to Mr. Lowell, and he didn't want to go alone for fear he would be tongue-tied.

Velda pounded on the door until Mr. Lowell opened it. There was no surprise in his face. Cady wondered if the man had been expecting them. Although he was quiet as usual, Mr. Lowell seemed more comfortable, easier in his actions. His face had slowed down—that was the way Cady would describe it. It was like a river that had washed away its banks and was now returning to its natural flow. Mr. Lowell examined the ribbon carefully when they gave it to him. "It's deserved," he said.

When Velda asked, he went out to the run and brought in Reynard. Then he made them hot tea and toast, and put it on a big tray with cheese and jam. They ate it in front of the fire. Cady lay on the floor beside the fox. He listened as the others talked. Velda laughed often, high and reedy. The man smiled once in a while, a vague, halfhearted smile. Cady waited for a special sign that things were different between the man and himself now.

Velda chattered about herself. "I've decided to stay," she announced to Mr. Lowell.

"She's got over her crazies about going home," Pete said. He tried to lean on one elbow while he fed himself toast.

"Are you going to live in this place forever?" Velda asked.

Mr. Lowell glanced at Cady as if measuring him.

"I mean, it looks so temporary here." Velda shrugged. "But nice."

"Life itself is temporary," Mr. Lowell said.

"I wouldn't mind staying in this house, especially in the summer." Velda jumped up and went to the window. She talked over her shoulder. "Maybe someday Pete and I could live here when you don't want it anymore."

"I'll bet Mr. Lowell stays here," Cady said. He put his teacup down carefully, without looking up.

"You going to stay?" Pete asked. When Mr. Lowell again didn't answer, Pete went on to talk more about the Science Fair and what they were going to do next year. "We might even use Reynard again, make a model of him, and start building it now. And I mean out of clay, or maybe Ingvald could help us carve one.

And maybe do all the animals that live out here in the woods."

"Who is going to catch them and hold them still?" Velda laughed. "But I think it would be nice to do birds. We see enough of those, and I can draw them. If you would help us again, Mr. Lowell. We could watch out your window without scaring them. The trees and the bushes are so close."

"Are you going to stay?" Cady spoke quietly, and looked directly at Mr. Lowell.

"I've been thinking about it."

It became quiet in the room, Pete still eating and Velda leaning on the windowsill looking out. The sun melted across the floor, coloring the fox golden. Cady petted it, rubbing behind its ears and running his hand across its head as Mr. Lowell had done. He liked the sensual feeling of stroking, the communion between the fox and himself. He felt the muscle and bones underneath, and the marvel of the heartbeat. The fox rested all of its weight against Cady. This is the way it is between the man and the fox, Cady thought.

He looked up at the man sprawled in his big chair, his head resting against the back. His eyes were half closed, hiding their piercing blue. His hair was smooth today, the color of mahogany, like Thea's. There was no doubt any longer for Cady. He had let this go on too long.

When they left that afternoon, the man walked to the door with them. "I'm coming back," Cady said. "Soon." The man nodded. He touched Cady on the arm, and pointed to the fox. It had followed him to the door. "We'll be expecting you."

That night Cady made himself wait until they had eaten supper, and he helped with the dishes. He brought in more wood for the fire. Thea sat at the card table typing. He sat down opposite her.

"I know who he is," he said.

"Who is he?" Thea's face was quiet.

"You know."

"Say it." Thea swept her hair back from her face.

"He's my father. He isn't dead."

"When did you get that idea?"

"At Christmas. The way we looked alike. The three of us sitting there, like we're tied together." Cady stopped to get his breath.

"Who am I, then?" Thea's eyes were bright.

"I'm not sure."

Thea seemed disappointed.

"I think I know."

"Yes?"

"That young brother you talked about was him."

"Yes."

"So that would make you my aunt." Cady felt a blush spreading over his face.

"That's right."

"Why did he pretend not to know me?"

"I don't know. . . ." Thea clasped her hands together, and stared down at her fingers as if she had not seen them before. "He was in a veterans' hospital. We hadn't known for a long time where he was. A doctor called me. When I brought him here, he acted as if he didn't know me. He didn't want to live here with me in this house. He was able to take care of himself, so we fixed up the old log house for him.

167

Ingvald helped me. He seemed contented enough, but he had erased the past. I tried to help him bring it back."

"You wanted me to help."

"And not to frighten him away."

"Why did he leave me?" Cady kept his voice even.

Thea concentrated on putting the cover over her typewriter. "Your mother died, and he didn't seem to know what else to do." She looked at him with troubled eyes.

"I didn't know she died when I was born. The Hawk told me. I couldn't help it."

"No, of course not." Thea looked at him, startled. "No one could help it. You sound like your father—he blamed himself. He joined the service and disappeared. We wrote to him but he never answered."

"I don't know why he left me behind. The Hawk said he was probably dead." Cady pressed his fist into his mouth. "I didn't want to believe it, that I didn't have anyone."

"Sometimes people get mixed up—in their heads. Being in the army didn't work, either. They said he had emotional problems. That's why he ended up in the vets' hospital. He said he didn't know who he was. That's what sorrow can do sometimes. He tried to shove it back, block it out. I guess if you don't want to face something, you won't until you're ready."

"I think he knew who I was. I saw the way he looked at me."

"It's hard to tell when he started to realize who you might be. He had been with me for almost two years when you came. He was beginning to come around, but he wouldn't talk about anything in the past. He never let on he had a child."

"Why didn't you just tell him who I was?" Cady spoke rapidly. He felt anger rising.

"I didn't want to shake him up." She carried the typewriter to the closet and shoved it in. "I thought we'd better go slowly. But I did want you to start out using your own name—your father's." Thea's voice was firm. "Edwin Lowell Myerling. He was always called Lowell. And then I thought everything would come about naturally—when you got to know each other."

"He's never called me by my name."

"He will." She picked up the sheets of paper on the table and stacked them, her hands flying. "And I didn't want that foolish Josephine to be able to trace you. I don't think she tried." Thea's eyes were bright. "They could accuse me of child stealing for what I've done. I had absolutely no legal right to you. Do you know what that means?"

"I had a father."

"Not until he was well. I wrote to Josephine after Christmas and told her that you were here. I explained about your father. She didn't answer."

"Did you say he was well enough to claim me?"

Thea nodded.

"I think he will. He isn't afraid to be around me now." Cady turned his face so Thea couldn't see it. "I just wanted him to like me."

"He will. You and I'll hang on to him."

In the night Thea came in and sat on his bed. Cady was almost asleep. In the dark cold, a web of light from the window touched his face. When she leaned over him, he opened his eyes. "Don't ever be angry with him," she said. "He couldn't stand it when your mother died. He thought it was his fault. They found him naked at your mother's grave. They put him in jail overnight. Those vicious people, Josephine and the family . . . they attacked him, slandered him, everything to humiliate him. That's when he disappeared."

"But why didn't you come after me sooner?" Cady twisted in bed to see Thea's face.

"I tried to get you when I came back from Texas. They kept you away from me, sending you from one family to another and never letting me see you. I never knew where you were—and I was a widow going to school. I always thought—one day." Thea tucked the covers up around his chin. She was shivering. "I kept in touch with Marrietta after she left home." Thea smiled when she spoke of Marrietta. "She was a little tyke, and lived down the road when I lived on the farm. But I hadn't heard from her for a long time until I received the frantic letter about you. I had believed you dead."

"Drowned?"

Thea nodded. She leaned her face in her hands to hide her tears. Cady thought it didn't seem like Thea to cry. She wasn't able to stop for several minutes. He touched her hand. Maybe she had waited too long to cry.

"But you never told me anything about him," he finally said.

"You had to work it out—the two of you. I didn't want anything to spoil it, so he would leave again. I didn't want to rush you—so you would turn away from us." She got up from the bed. "I had to just let it happen." She blew her nose and wiped her eyes. "The way it would, when the time was right. I thought—you getting to know each other should come first. Then learning he was your father would come easier. I thought in time you would recognize each other."

"I never knew what he looked like. I used to make him up—how he would look."

"Are you disappointed?"

"No. He's like you."

"I was hoping you would run across each other, but I was never sure how he would act."

"It's funny how he treated me."

"It was hard for you both." Thea leaned over him. She had stopped crying. She kissed him on the cheek before she left.

Cady called after her. "You don't need to worry about him getting away now. I'll hang on to him so he can't."

26

Later in the night the rain woke Cady. In the winter? Then he remembered it was the third week of March, and the rain came with the wind. But in the morning the ground was covered with snow. The jack pines, like Christmas trees, were decorated with crystals, and it was winter again.

As soon as Cady and Thea had eaten breakfast, he hurried to help her with the dishes. He waited patiently until their Sunday dinner was eaten. He brought in enough wood to last the day. Once he asked her suddenly, "Will they arrest me because I'm not drowned?" They both laughed over that, Thea until she had tears on her cheeks. When he began to bundle up and put on his high boots, Thea knew where he was going but didn't offer to go along. "It's better the two of you," she said.

The ground had frozen hard again under the snow, and in places it was slick, but the snow was no more than two or three inches deep, except for the deep snowbanks that had not melted away in the rain.

Cady sensed something was wrong as soon as the man opened the door. Mr. Lowell seemed to start talking in the middle of a thought. "Last night it was raining." Cady nodded. "I woke up and I heard it on the roof. Reynard was restless, and I put him in the run. Then I went back to sleep. I forgot him. I slept like I was a child again. I had a sense of great peace, of being warm and dry."

"I like to listen to the rain when I'm in bed. It always puts me to sleep, too," Cady said.

The man nodded absentmindedly, then abruptly he changed. "When I remembered and went out early this morning, Reynard was gone. The padlock had been broken on the gate. I've spent the morning looking for him."

Cady thought for a moment. "Could an animal do it?"

"A human animal."

"Why would they?" Then came the painful thought that perhaps he, Cady, had led them to the fox because of his science project and all the publicity given to Reynard. He felt his face flush. He had such a hurt in his throat, it was hard for him to speak. "We should keep looking. I'll go with you."

They went up the cliff where Cady had found the trap. There was no sign of anything, no tracks, nothing. They called as they walked. Cady peered ahead into the icy stillness. He looked for a flash of copper or bronze. He wanted to see the fox leaping and running. They separated for a while and went in different directions. Wherever Cady saw a mound or hole he pounced on it, throwing something into the hole, or

prodding for a trap. After an hour he was getting cold. Then he heard his name being called. Mr. Lowell came through the trees alone.

"I think we'd better head home. Maybe he's come back," he said.

But they walked to the cliff once again, and down past the ledges. Cady thought it was good that they were together when they found Reynard. The fox lay under a tree, partially covered by snow. It looked as if it was running, its hind feet stretched out. The fox might have been jumping, whirling, dancing. The grace was there in the still body.

"He could still be alive," Cady said.

Mr. Lowell knelt beside the fox. He put his hand on its head as though he were patting it. The smudged ears and nose were stark against the snow. "He isn't," he said.

On the fox's chest, where the fur was shaded to the palest, golden yellow, was a tiny hole, red rimmed. The man touched it gently and smoothed the fur around it. Cady put his hand beside the man's and stroked the fur. "You see, he really is rust colored," Mr. Lowell said. "It's when he moves that he changes color, except for his belly."

When he turned to the man, Cady's face was streaming with tears. "I caused it," he said.

"Nonsense," the man said brusquely. "You mustn't say that. It was the man with the trap. One way or the other." He let Cady cry against his chest, but he didn't hold him. "Sometimes there is no way to protect yourself."

When they raised the fox to carry it home, Cady saw a puddle of blood underneath it. Under the large tree near Mr. Lowell's door they took turns digging the grave until the hole was deep enough. They wrapped an old jacket around the fox and they covered him with the frozen chunks of earth.

Cady followed the man into the house. Mr. Lowell made coffee, and they sat across from each other. It was hard to talk. The fox was not mentioned again. Cady sat there until he could stand it no longer. He braced himself against the chair, his heels flat on the floor. "I know who you are," he said to Mr. Lowell.

At first the man did not appear to have heard Cady. He turned his head so that his face was hidden. It was an awkward angle, and the man had to be doing it deliberately. He sat so still that even though he couldn't see, Cady knew the man had not flicked an eyelash or licked his lips. It was as close as a man might come to death, Cady thought, to remain so quiet while still breathing. Cady looked at the man's hands. They rested, one on each knee. The fingers were long and slender, curved now, as if reaching, but carved from stone. His father needed to be comforted.

"I'm sorry about the fox. I think I know how you feel inside."

His father turned and looked at him then. He nodded. Abruptly he said, "We haven't eaten." Cady went with him to the kitchen. They fried bacon and eggs. Cady opened a jar of applesauce, and poured more coffee. They ate in silence. It was much later when the man spoke again. "Why do you come so often to see me? I'm not good company."

"You're my father," Cady said. His breath came in a rush. "I learn from you."

"I hope it's good, what you learn." There was a

skeptical look on the man's face. "What is it that you learn?"

"About you . . ." Cady's voice tapered off. "Why you act like you do." He darted a quick glance at his father. "I wanted to know why you would not recognize me as your boy."

"I don't have a boy."

"Thirteen years ago you did."

"They both died. I caused it."

"The boy lived."

"I never saw him."

"Why didn't you?"

His father's lips pressed into a straight line.

"He didn't die."

"They told me that you weren't my son—that I was a killer."

"I kept waiting for you. And then Josephine said you were dead. That's what she told me."

"I've not done much for anyone. Why should I mess up your life?"

"It was messed up when I was born."

"So you're ashamed of me?"

"No. I feel sorry for you. Thea said you wouldn't like that."

"Thea has always thought she knew what I was thinking."

"Maybe she did. Some of the time I think I know."

"With me you can't be sure, though, can you?"

"I dreamed about you sometimes," Cady said. "I never dreamed about my mother."

"I've dreamed about her, quite often." The man studied Cady's face. "Your smile is the same. . . ." He broke off, embarrassed. "I never go back to her grave.

I can't. Her soul is not there. She's not there." He put his face in his hands, and sat quiet for several minutes. When he looked up at Cady, his expression had changed. "She has forgiven me, or you wouldn't be here. That's true, isn't it? That's the way it seems to me." His eyes were muddied now, no longer ice blue or fierce. His voice was clinging, not something Cady could push away. His father seemed to have slipped back into the past.

"Everyone has forgiven you," Cady said. "There is nothing to worry about." Cady remembered what Thea had said about sorrow, that it does strange things.

"I never ran away from your mother. She went with me, you know. Wherever I was, she was. The soul lives forever."

Cady's eyes wandered to the empty place at the man's knee where the fox had sat.

"You'll miss the fox," he said. "Do you believe it has a soul?"

"Some say they don't. I believe otherwise."

"Then he will stay here with you."

"In some ways, yes. The woods is a good reminder."

"But you'll be lonely."

The man sighed wearily, and pushed his plate back so he could lean on his elbows. Cady saw that the fine lines around his eyes and mouth had deepened. "I will be lonely," he said.

"I was lonely, too," Cady said, "but there are others." Cady tried to laugh. "All you have to do is claim them."

"You think so? Claim is an odd way to put it."

Cady struggled for the right words. "You can't claim them like you would a place. They are not a property.

178

But they will give you something back, like the fox did."

The man's eyes widened, surprised, as if he were taking in Cady for the first time. Cady was surprised, too, because he was trying to say all the things that Thea had told him—a place can't love you back, but another person can.

Then his father began to talk. He talked on and on, and Cady listened. He talked of things he hadn't spoken of for a long time, mostly about his young wife, Cady's mother. When Cady was ready to go home, his father gripped his hand and hung on. "It's good for me here. Maybe it's good you came. I had forgotten so many things." He followed Cady out, and stood in the doorway with a hand on either side, as if bracing himself.

Cady looked back at his father. The light from the room shone out around him, traveling across the snow, making a single shadow.

27

Thea was sad when Cady told her about the fox's death. She quickly asked how her brother was, and she went to see him the next day.

But Thea and Cady went separately on their visits to him. Thea had said, "We won't rush him." Cady stopped each night on the way home from school that week. His father had hot tea or coffee waiting for him. Sometimes they hardly spoke. It was more a need to be together, for Cady to be near him. Cady still called him Mr. Lowell, feeling awkward at calling him father.

On the following Sunday, Cady asked his father to come to the big house for the day. Thea had planned it to be a family dinner, the three of them; then Velda and Pete turned up in the morning to bring cheese and milk for them, so she told Pete to go after Ingvald. "We want things to be as natural as possible," she said. And it turned out that way. Velda helped, setting the table in the front room and mashing the potatoes, and chattering away like a song sparrow. She cried hard when she and Cady talked about the fox, but when he told her who Mr. Lowell was, she flushed, and a knowing look crossed her face. She had guessed a long time ago, she said.

Cady greeted his father at the door. He felt shy with him. And at first his father was stiff and self-conscious, as he had been at Christmas, saying few words. Ingvald sat in a chair close to Cady's father. He told him about the wheat crop, and the pair of kids his old nanny gave birth to three days ago, and how he couldn't get Velda and Pete to leave them alone. Then suddenly Ingvald turned serious. Leaning forward and putting his hand on Lowell's knee, he said, "My tenant is moving, traps, guns and all." When Cady asked if he was the one who might have killed Reynard, Ingvald shrugged. "Who knows for sure? I can't prove it."

Cady looked quickly at his father. The man shifted in his chair and stretched his legs out full length in front of him. Cady thought it was as if he had answered with his body—a sigh of relief.

The six of them sat around the table—like a family reunion, Cady thought. Ingvald was quite noisy, insisting everyone eat some of his goat cheese. Thea kept them busy with more and more food: "Lowell's favorite—breaded porkchops," she said, "with sweet potatoes and apple salad." She saved the best for last, bringing in a huge coconut pie. They sat for quite a long time at the table. Velda poured them more coffee. Once when Cady looked up at Thea she was smiling at him. The powerful set of her jaws seemed more pronounced tonight; her hair swept around her face like a dark flame and her eyes shone. She sat erect, her head turned gracefully. Cady touched her wrist. Thea with her strength had pounded cement into the cracks, so nothing could fall apart for any of them. It was solid like Cady wanted it, something he could press against, feel with his whole body, and it wouldn't break or change.

After Ingvald left with Pete and Velda, the three of them sat around the fire. A fierce wind outside tossed sleet against the windows and caused the flames to leap. Thea talked about their childhood. When there was a silence, she prodded Lowell to answer Cady's questions about their mother and father.

Later, after the sleet had stopped and Lowell was leaving, Thea with sudden emotion kissed him on the cheek. Cady touched his father, at first shyly, then his arms went around his neck and he hugged him. Cady was startled to see his father's face so open, infinitely tender, Cady's loneliness and pain shared.

The spring came late. It had snowed the night before, even though it was the middle of April. Cady and his father walked out past the pond, along the trails that Cady had marked. The blue jays were calling, and the breeze through the jack pines sounded to Cady like the high notes of a mouth organ. He saw it first—a shadow, beautiful and lithe, red as a copper penny, before it was lost in the trees. Its tracks led Cady and his father off to the wildest part of the woods, past the knoll, to a woodchuck's den. In the opening, Cady saw two young kits fighting over a rabbit skin. At the sound of a high-pitched bark from the vixen, they disappeared into the den.

"You see, nature has its own rhythm," Cady's father said.

"They look like Reynard."

"They are probably his kits." The man smiled to himself.

Then quietly, so thay wouldn't disturb the foxes, Cady and his father turned and started home.

Forrest Aguirre was born in Wiesbaden, Germany, the son of an Air Force Sergeant. After living in five different countries and roaming the world like a gypsy, he finally settled in Madison, Wisconsin with his wife and four children. He holds a bachelor's degree in Humanities from BYU and a Master's in African History from the University of Wisconsin-Madison. His short fiction has appeared in over fifty venues and his editorial work has been recognized with a World Fantasy Award. He is best bribed with very expensive dark chocolate, herbal tea, role playing games, books, swords, early modern silver coins, Badgers regalia, and canoes.